ACE OF WANDS

BRIAN A. HILL

THE ACE OF WANDS

Copyright © 2016 Brian A. Hill

ISBN - 978-0-9977557-0-1

Cover design and Interior Layout by Sean Keenan

Edited by Wooodbine Publishing

Publisher: Woodbine Publishing LLC

www.brianahill.com

ACE OF WANDS

BRIAN A. HILL

PROLOGUE

The Ace of Wands is an ancient symbol representing a gift of illumination from the heavens, which guides its recipient through an arduous journey. This gift of illumination must however, be accompanied by courageous action to secure the journey's reward.

CHAPTER 1

It had been a long sleepless rainy night. By 5 a.m. I was in the damp garage pounding the guts out of a seventy pound punching bag I called Henry. Employing Henry was the most cost effective and efficient way I'd found to work off my inner turmoil. On that soggy morning, Henry worked overtime.

After my pugilistic therapy and a couple cups of coffee, I went to Ethan's room to wake him. I laughed when I saw his ten-year old frame curled asleep in the middle of the bed with all the bedcovers on the floor but with his cherished baseball glove on his hand, tucked safely in the curve of his belly. The kid didn't do anything or go anywhere without his baseball glove.

Such a sweet picture of innocence, it was a shame to wake him. When my gentle approach of rubbing his shoulder failed to stir him, I tugged a little on his baseball glove but that didn't do the trick either. A harder tug met with the tightening of his grip. Faker.

I was onto his game. My third tug, stronger and more decisive freed the glove from his hold but my victory faced instant retaliation. He sprang on me, like a hungry monkey jumps on a banana tree, and with a lightning move he snatched his beloved glove from my grasp.

"Once again, my glove is safe from the evil empire," he roared.

"Is that what I am, the evil empire?"

"Nah, not really dad. You're really pretty cool."

"You're just saying that because you want me to feed you."

"That's not true," he said seriously but then laughed again. "Yes it is. Yes it is."

"Even if it is true, I'm still going to feed you because I love you. So what's it going to be this morning?"

"French toast, please. Today I have baseball practice, so I need extra energy.

"You'd better hope it stops raining, so practice doesn't get rained out. How many pieces?"

"Four please."

"Four? You must really be hungry."

"I'm starving," he declared and then jumped off bed, put his black baseball glove on his golden head and sauntered into the bathroom.

As I walked around the room and picked up the scattered bedcovers, I paused and remembered renovating his room. Five years earlier, when I bought the house from Frank Mangello, the room was half the size and didn't have a bathroom. Building the bathroom proved a nightmare because all the plumbing lines were on the other side of the house. I did the construction mostly alone. It was a tough job but in the end it was well worth it because he loves his boy cave. My plan was for him to have it a long, long time. That was still the plan, despite the current situation.

Twenty minutes later, fully dressed with his baseball glove snug on his head, Ethan hopped up on the kitchen counter.

"Perfect timing, your breakfast is ready."

"Hey dad, since it's raining let's call the sun room the rain room and eat in there."

"Sounds good to me."

He took his French toast, went into the rain room and plopped down in front of the television.

"And please, best father in the whole wide world, can I watch tv while I eat?"

I laughed and said, "That's funny."

"But…but why not? I don't get it," he grumbled.

I peered into his blue eyes but didn't say a word."

"I hate it when you give me that look."

"Good, it saves me words and time." I playfully knocked his glove off his head and said, "And, I still love you."

***

At 8 a.m., we ran through the rain and hopped into my twelve year old Toyota Highlander. I turned the key in the ignition, it whined a sad song but didn't start. I turned it again, same song. After a third unsuccessful try, I got under the hood, cleaned the cable connections and hoped that would do the trick.

It didn't.

"Dad, we need a new car. This one is on its last whine. Hey, can we get a sports car instead of another SUV?"

My patience was thin, with the old Highlander and with Ethan's observation. Both smarted because of my inability to either fix the Highlander or buy a new one.

"We need a SUV for two reasons. The more important reason to you is, so we can haul your teammates and their equipment around to your games. And second, I need it when I'm showing properties to my clients. So buddy, I'm afraid there's no sports car in our near future."

With an understanding look on his face he said. "Do you think we get this one started today so I can at least get to school?"

"I'm working on it." I gave it another crank. This time, luck was with me.

Five minutes later, because of the rain we were stuck in even slower than normal traffic. I learned a long time ago that people who live in sunny Sarasota, Florida sooner or later forget how to drive in the rain. So for the next fifteen minutes, we crawled along the half-mile on Osprey Ave. to Southside Elementary School. I reminded myself that one of the most important reasons I chose our home was so Ethan would be in the Southside district. It was a smart decision.

We arrived at school ten minutes late but we were certainly not alone. I inched up to the drop off spot. Ethan enthusiastically grabbed his glove, carefully put on his baseball hat and apathetically picked up his books. He opened the door, got out, closed it behind him and started to walk away. That surprised me. But in the next second, he turned and with a big smile on his face, ran back to me and climbed back in the Highlander.

"Fooled you, didn't I?" he said laughing.

"Yes, you did buddy." I laughed with him.

He gave me a big hug and a kiss and trotted back along his way. I watched him head into school. He was getting big. Time had gone by fast.

Slowly I pulled up to the stop sign at the school exit. A book Ethan forgot fell off the front seat. Without a car behind me, I picked it up and then checked the flow of oncoming traffic. It was clear, so I thought. When I accelerated on to Webber Street, a black convertible Mercedes came out of the ethers, whizzed by me and missed slamming into me by inches. I hit the brake hard and strangled the steering wheel. I was pissed and needed to find my breath, to calm down. Contemplating what happened, I wasn't sure if it was a bad omen or if I was lucky he missed me. I hoped for the good luck. I needed it badly.

CHAPTER 2

The rain had lessened but the traffic still crept, so by the time I got to Moe's Place I was fifteen minutes late. The large wooden front door reminded me of a gate to a medieval fortress and it felt as heavy. Inside, the joint was full of characters that resembled an open casting call for a Dirty Harry movie. It was obvious. Moe's Place was where the underworld and the cops came to eat breakfast. And there in the middle of the drama, Mickey Blackburn was holding court. But that was no surprise to me.

When Blackie saw me, he pointed to an empty table off in a corner, next to a window. It looked like the table was reserved but I didn't spot a sign. I met him at the table.

"Well, well, well, if it's not Jake Shaw. It's about time ya get here. I was beginning to wonder if ya got kidnapped."

"Blackie, it's Sarasota not New York."

"Yeah, yeah I know but it ain't easy shakin' old

habits."

"Is that why you hang out in this place? Does it remind you of New York?"

"Yeah sorta. I like mixin' with the people and bull shittin' with my comrades in blue. Some days I really miss the job." He laughed. "But not enough to want to go back. Being a retired homicide captain has a nice ring to it. Especially the retired part."

"No one would ever think that you're a retired cop. You look more like a perp. Especially with those tattoos on your forearms."

"Hey, go easy on my art work," he laughed again. Blackie laughed a lot.

A hardcore biker walked past our table, "Hey Blackie, you coming tonight?"

"For sure Willie. Tonight at eight."

"You two ladies going dancing tonight?" I asked.

"Not my type." He shook his head and took a swig of coffee. "There's a card game and I aim to make some good dough tonight."

"I've known you almost four years but I never stop learning things about you. Like this joint, Moe's Place. How come we've never come here before? I like it."

He avoided the question but offered, "Hey, what's not to like."

Like, wasn't the exact word I had in mind but it did entertain me. It had about a couple dozen four top tables filling the single room. There wasn't a matching set of chairs in the entire place. The only thing the chairs had in common was that they were all wooden with various colors and degrees of paint on them. The faded blue walls were covered with anything that could hang on them, including a stuffed hissing bobcat, an old rusted saw and a large picture of Elvis. Whatever could cover space, found a home.

"Food's good here and cheap too. I like a good deal," he said.

The waitress came to the table, took our orders and before I could get settled, she was back with our food. For that kind of service, Moe must really like Blackie.

"How'd the Yankees do last night?" I asked.

"Ah, my Yankees I love my Yankees. They won again. Only been a couple of weeks into the season but they're off to a good start. They're on a roll. I'm a happy guy." He turned and looked around to see if anybody could hear. "And here's something I don't tell to no one, so consider yourself special. Ya hear me?" He looked around the room again then leaned into me. He waited for a second as if to make sure he really wanted to say what he was going to tell me. "My father, may he rest in peace, loved the New York Yankees so much that he named me after his favorite Yankee of all time."

"Yogi Berra?" I joked.

"You're funny Jake, real funny." He smiled and continued, "Not only was Mickey Mantle my father's favorite player but he became mine too. I keep my name thing private. Just don't want people knowing it but for some reason I tell you." He shrugged his shoulders. "So keep it quiet. Ya hear me?"

"I hear you, Mickey Mantle Blackburn. I hear you."

We sat for a few minutes in quiet and ate our breakfast. I glanced out the window, the rain had stopped and I felt relieved.

"Now Jake, tell me about my favorite topic in your life. How's Camille? Ya getting any pressure to a ... ya know do the deed, walk down the aisle?"

"She's fine. We're doing fine. And sort of, yes."

"No shit. She's puttin' heat on ya. How you doing with that?"

"To be honest..."

"No, lie to me Jake, lie to me."

I laughed at him. He was about as subtle as a freight train pulling into a small village but Blackie would be the guy I'd want to protect my back in a dark alley. And physically, he was about as large as that freight train.

"I'm uneasy with it," I said.

"Are ya nuts? She's a keeper, a real keeper. Do anything ya need to do to keep her. Do ya hear? Do ya?"

"It's not that easy."

"What do ya mean, it's not that easy? Sure it is. Ya, just do it."

"This isn't a Nike commercial Blackie, it's real life." He got my point and sat back.

"Jake, I admire a guy who knows how to brush back a batter when he's crowding the plate. Okay, I'll shut up. And, just for the record, I think you're capable of throwin' the heat at somebody when you need to."

He sat back in his chair, crossed his arms and clammed up. I made him wait for a moment before I continued.

"Here's the deal. My business has been terrible for almost two years and money has been pouring from my bank account like water out of cracked aquarium.

But today finally, finally I could get a break."

"How come?"

"I got three deals in the pipeline. One is happening today, if the weather cooperates. Then I got another one, a sizeable deal that looks solid and could close inside a month, maybe six weeks. The last one's about fifty-fifty but could close quickly too, if it happens."

"Sounds good buddy boy."

"I sure hope so. It's been rough and I'm way behind. It's not fun, to say the least."

"In the old days Jake, when your were pitchin', I'm sure you got yourself behind in the count with a batter and still got him out. Am I right?

"Sure."

"Same thing here. It's just been a long, tough couple of innings but you'll get out of this jam."

"That's my plan. Nevertheless, this is no time for me to take on added responsibility of a marriage."

Blackie had his detective face on, "Gotta a question for you?"

"Shoot."

"Does Camille know what you're goin' through?"

"No. I don't talk about it with her. I just can't. You're the only one I told. So now we're even, Mickey Mantle Blackburn."

"Hey, I knew you were havin' troubles. Didn't know the details but knew somethin' didn't smell good."

"What do you mean?"

"Two things. One the economy sucks. And two, signs. I didn't spend those years lookin' at clues for nothin'. But now… I wanna hear about today's deal."

" It's simple but substantial. There's a couple

moving to Sarasota, nice couple. They want a condo downtown facing the water. They got cash and can close immediately. I got three to show them and all of them meet their requirements. It should be an easy deal for a change."

I glanced out the window. The sun was pushing through the clouds. I felt lucky for the first time in a long time.

Blackie didn't say anything to me. He sat as if he was going over the clues at a crime scene. The waitress came over with check. Blackie grabbed it. "Breakfast is on me."

As he fumbled with his cash, I noticed an old cuckoo clock on the blue wall. It was time for me to go.

"Hey I have to run to meet my clients. I'll catch you later. Thanks for the grub."

"No problem. Go make some money," he said without looking up.

"That's my plan."

CHAPTER 3

Charlie's Newsstand was only ten minutes from Moe's Place but it could have been in a different country. It was a high-end cafe that carried magazines and newspapers from countries all over the globe. The clientele was as erudite as Moe's customers were street tough.

I had fifteen minutes before the Berks were to arrive, so I got a small decaf and grabbed a seat by the door. Taking my first sip, I spotted Frank Mangello and another man heading toward the door. Mangello had always been a friend but when he saw me, his face turned sour and I quickly surmised his look. I was already two months late on the mortgage he held on my house and in a week it would be three. As he approached the door, I started to get up to greet him.

"Don't get up Jake."

I was already up. I shook his reluctant hand.

"Good morning Frank. Staying dry?"

"Barely, but I think it's done raining for the day, at least I hope so."

"Me too. I'm showing property," I said with an air of confidence.

"Good for you Jake." He hesitated. "Listen Jake, we need to talk but right now I have to go to meeting. I'll call you tomorrow. I hope you have a successful day."

Mangello had never been curt before. He'd always been a wordy guy. For the five years he's held my mortgage I've had an easy, affable relationship with him, even when I told him I was having trouble with my payment, he was kind and generous. Something changed and it wasn't good.

I sat back down and took a swig of coffee. It soothed my anxiety. My mind went to the Berks and my confidence rose because I knew the Berks were serious buyers with ready cash and they'd be there in a few minutes. I'd show them the properties, they'd fall in love with one of them, I'd get them under contract and in two or three weeks, their deal would close and I'd make good with Mangello. I took a deep, easy breath.

In the time before the Berks arrived, I reviewed the property listings, confident that each property met their criteria exactly. I lined up the order of viewing for optimum efficiency and double-checked the contracts.

The only contact I've had with the Berks had been on the telephone but we talked so many times it seemed like they were old friends. I looked forward to meeting them in person. I checked the weather and saw the sun out. I felt good. All systems were a go.

***

Thirty minutes later there was no sign of the Berks. I would've called them but we only talked on their land line so I didn't have a cell number for them. I couldn't believe I was going to get stood up. I thought of Mangello and my stomach tightened. I needed this deal big time. A minute later my phone rang. I took a deep breath.

"Jake Shaw speaking."

"Hey Jake, Jim Berk here. Sorry about the delay. We've been sitting on I-75 in the middle of a traffic jam for almost an hour but we're moving now. We're just north of Northport and we must have been in a dead zone because I couldn't get even one bar on my phone."

I relaxed a bit. "You're right Jim. There is a dead zone in that area."

"Mary says hello, Jake."

"Hello to Mary."

"Jake, while we were sitting in traffic Mary and I were discussing how much we love Sarasota. There's no doubt about that. Sarasota is the place we want to be. We spent the last few days with Mary's sister in Fort Myers, and although it's lovely in it's own way, we much prefer Sarasota."

Jim's words were dancing in my ears.

"You are so right Jim, Sarasota is a rare jewel."

"Like I said, Mary and I have no doubt about Sarasota."

My confidence rose. I sipped my coffee.

"When we were in Fort Myers, we realized that Mary's sister is not doing well. Her health is failing much quicker than we realized. And since her husband's death, she needs more help than ever. Mary and I both felt that with Sarasota being an hour or less away, we could manage the distance."

"I understand your concern Jim. Family is prime. And you're right, Sarasota is only a short hop to Fort Myers so when you need to, you can be down there quickly."

"I'm sorry Jake, I don't think I'm being clear. We're still on I-75 but we've turned around heading south, back to Fort Myers. While we were sitting in traffic, Mary and I decided that her sister needs us more than we need Sarasota. And you're right Jake, Sarasota is just a short hop from Fort Myers. We can easily drive up when we want to. There's a condo for rent in her sister's building and we've decided to take it for a year."

I was stunned. Stunned. Heat rushed through my veins, my stomach tightened, my free hand made a fist and my throat clamped shut. I couldn't find a word.

"Jake? Jake? Did we lose you? Did we hit another dead zone?"

I regained minimal composure. "I'm here Jim. You probably hit a dead spot. I can hear you loud and clear now."

"Quickly before we do get to that dead zone, Mary and I want to thank you for your effort for us. And we want to apologize to you for any inconvenience we've caused you. But sometimes the ball bounces in a different direction as it did with Mary's sister."

Inconvenience? Inconvenience? This wasn't just inconvenience, it was disaster. Absolute disaster. The ball didn't bounce in a different direction, it bounced out of the ball park. I could've chewed a 2x4 yellow pine stud.

Jim Berk continued, "However, when this situation changes, we absolutely want to live in Sarasota and we sincerely want to work with you. In the meantime, when we visit Sarasota, we'd like to meet you and take you to dinner. We'd like that. Would that be possible?"

I thought about the unpaid bills on my kitchen table. I barely heard a word he said. But I tried.

"Absolutely. I'd like that too," I said. But what I'd really wanted to do was sell him a damn condo. "It'd be good to put faces on the voices I've been hearing. And you know there are plenty of fine restaurants here." I could hardly get the words out.

"Jake, I think we're about to……"

"Hit the dead zone." I said and waited a minute, then hung up.

My mind whirled like a torn movie ticket blowing in the wind. I couldn't believe it. Nothing… Nothing…. Nothing was working. I wanted to shoot somebody. But who? Me?

My body felt like lead and I sat slumped in a timeless blur until I heard a gravelly voice.

"You okay?"

I glanced up and saw an elderly man looking down at me. I mumbled a lie. "Sure. Sure. I'm fine."

The old man nodded to the floor beside me. I followed his eyes to an empty cup and the puddle of coffee at my feet. I had no idea I dropped my coffee. "Damn it." What else could go wrong?

"Need help?" he asked.

"No, I got it. No problem."

"Sure?"

I looked up at him again. He was a big guy. Had to be 6'4" and at least 220 pounds, probably in his 70's. He had a strong weathered look but with the clear blue eyes of a younger man. My sense was that when he was younger, he was guy you didn't want to mess with.

"Yeah, I'm hanging in there. Just lost a deal."

He nodded with understanding.

"The school of hard knocks." I said, feigning to be polite.

"The tuition can be costly. Better to learn on someone else's dollar," he said.

He seemed grounded, in the present moment, solid like an oak tree. I sensed he'd been there, gone through it, and came out on the other side, smarter and tougher.

"How does one learn on someone else's dollar?" I asked.

"Observe. Listen."

"That's fine if you have someone you want to listen to and if he wants to share things with you but what I mostly hear is the gerbil wheel turning around in my own mind."

"Tough cycle to break."

This guy intrigued me. I wanted to hear more but he said, "Got to go. Have a better day."

"Thanks."

I collected the soggy napkins I used to clean up my coffee and threw them in the trash can. I remembered my phone call with Jim Berk, my quick interchange with Mangello and quickly forgot the old man. I sat back in the chair and took a deep breath and tried to get centered. It took a few minutes for my attitude to become more positive and with it came a rush of adrenaline. I was determined to get out of this mess. There was no way I was going to lose this battle. That wasn't going to happen. No way. No matter what it took. No matter what...

CHAPTER 4

"Dad, are you sure she got home today?"

I chuckled at his impatience.

"Ethan, for the fourth time, yes I'm sure she got home today."

He plopped down on the living room couch next to me and snuggled against my side. I wrapped my arm around his neck.

"Don't you remember when I picked you up from school, I told you I talked to her this afternoon?"

"Yeah, yeah I remember but its after six and she's supposed to be here by now."

"Seems like you missed her."

"Well she's cool dad. Really cool."

"I'm glad you think so. I think so too. Big time."

"When I get older I want somebody just like Camille."

"That's sounds good to me. But ---."

"But what?"

"There might be only one of her."

"Then we need to clone her."

I rustled his hair with my hand.

"Patience grasshopper. She'll be here any moment."

He got up and went to the front window. "Look! Look! You must be psychic. She's pulling in the driveway right now."

He bolted out the front door, ran to her rag-top yellow Jeep, climbed over the door and gave her a huge hug before she could get out of her seat. I went to the front porch and watched them walk hand in hand toward me. She looked good, like water in a desert. My breath deepened and my eyes moistened.

We met at the open door with my arms wide open. Without a word she accepted my invitation, folded into my chest and my arms closed around her. Her familiar sweet scent was intoxicating. I missed her more than I realized. I gently raised her face. She offered her lips to me. I kissed them softly and inhaled her breath. Nothing in the world was sweeter to me than Camille. Nothing.

"Come on you love birds. I'm hungry. I want some pizza. Stop the smooching and feed this poor kid before he starves to death."

We laughed at Ethan and rushed toward him and tickled him into almost tears. "Okay, okay, okay. I surrender," he screamed.

I let go of him, turned toward Camille and gave her another hug. "I really missed you honey."

"I really missed you too." She squeezed me again. "I had plenty of time on the flight to think and, and...I need to talk about some things."

"Sure honey. No problem." I had a good idea what

she wanted to talk about.

Ethan's hunger was persistent.

"Come on people. I'm starving."

As the three of us piled into Camille's Jeep, I noticed her hair. "I like your new haircut."

"I got it done in small place in Nice. It's called a 'flirty side swept pixie cut.' I was wondering if and when you'd notice," she said with a smile.

"Honey, my heart was pounding so much when I saw you, my eyes were too blurry to see clearly."

"You are so smooth Jake Shaw, so smooth."

"Pizza please. Please. Please. Please start the car," came Ethan's plea.

***

When we walked into Antonio's Restaurant, Tony the jovial owner of the restaurant, greeted us with a huge smile. It felt like being invited into the home of a dear friend in a Tuscan village.

"It's so long since I see you. Did you getta married and have long honeymoon?" Tony impishly inquired.

Camille laughed. "I wish," she said, "A long honeymoon sounds divine. But no, no, we've just been busy with family matters."

"Ah family. Family is what it's all about. And I know you are a family. Married or not," Tony offered. "Letta me take you to your favorite booth."

Tony and I walked behind Camille and Ethan. He whispered to me, "You marry her soon eh? Before she can get away. You a lucky man."

I smiled but didn't reply. Of course, I knew I was a

lucky man.

Our normal table was in a more private section of the restaurant. Five booths were tucked away in the far corner, away from the main dining room. On the table, white paper served both as the table cloth and drawing paper. A bucket of crayons awaited the eager young artist. Ethan loved the décor. Blessed with his mother's artistic ability, he happily grabbed a red crayon and went immediately to work.

"So you gonna have your usual? Two chiantis, Pepsi, and a large pizza with onions, green peppers and tomatoes. Right?" Tony asked.

"I don't know how you remember that," I said.

"It's cause I like you." Again he flashed his impish smile.

The wine and soda arrived quickly. "So other than your new haircut, did you experience anything exciting while you visited your mother in France? Did you go anywhere interesting with her?"

"Of course, we went to the Matisse Chapel in Nice. I hadn't been there in years. I simply adore Matisse and his amazing use of color. He totally understood the powerful affect colors have in our life."

"I too, totally understand the powerful affects color has in my life," I said with small smile.

"You do? Are you kidding me, Jake Shaw? We never talked about color before."

"I most certainly do. Like the mesmerizing affect those stunning jade eyes of yours have on me, especially offset by your luxurious dark, chocolate hair and your olive skin. Your color inspires me."

"Jake, I'm serious."

"So am I dear. So am I."

"You flatter me so well."

"I only speak the truth. You are more beautiful than any Matisse painting. Or any painting for that matter."

I swirled the red wine in the glass. "I drink to the work of art you are."

We clinked our glasses and each took a drink.

"And… I am glad you enjoyed your hometown."

"Jake, it was better than I remembered. I learned so much. More than ever, I realized that Matisse really wasn't an impressionist, or a neo-impressionist or a cubist or anything else. Matisse created his own style and that's what I strive to do. Like a writer strives to find his voice, I want to find my painting style."

Ethan chimed in, "Hey what about my style?" He pointed to the colored drawing he finished. "What do you think of this?"

On the table was a drawing of the three of us with a caption below that read. 'A Family.'

"That is incredible Ethan. I'm amazed by it," Camille said. "From my trained eye, I say you're quite the realist. That is a highly accurate depiction of each of us. Including your self-portrait. Maybe someday we can paint together. Would you like to do that with me?"

"You bet I would. When can we do it?"

"I'll check my schedule and then arrange a time with your father for us to create our masterpieces. Maybe even your father will join us."

"Wait a minute," I said. "Two artists gracing this family is a blessing. I'm not about to ruin the level of quality."

"Excuse me, did I hear you say family?" Camille questioned. "Not quite yet big boy." She laughed. "We'll have that conversation later."

Our pizza arrived and we all quickly grabbed a slice. Ethan wasn't the only one hungry and it didn't take long to finish the eight pieces.

"Can I have one more Pepsi before we go?" Ethan asked.

"How many have you had?"

"Two."

"I'm sorry buddy, but it's getting late, you have school tomorrow and you still have to take a shower. With all that caffeine and sugar you'll never get to sleep. You want water?"

He made a dejected face. "Yes please."

***

At home, after I helped Ethan with his shower and got him into bed, I walked into the living room and saw Camille snuggled up under the throw blanket on the couch sound asleep. I was disappointed there wouldn't be any love making but I breathed a sigh of relief when I realized that our talk would be postponed too. But it wasn't exactly an even trade off.

I gently stroked her smooth cheek. She awoke easily and sat up.

"You came light tonight. Should I assume you're not staying?" I pouted to apply guilt.

"No baby, not tonight. I know it's been awhile but this jet lag is starting to get to me and I need to get up for a meeting in the morning. But please believe me, I miss you too. Terribly."

She looked up at me and offered her lips. I bent down, and kissed her firmly. After a moment, I reluctantly pulled back knowing this was not going anywhere tonight. After two years with her, I knew I wanted to stop before my jets got too revved up. She stood up straightening her clothes. My jets sadly simmered.

"I want to remind you that I have two tickets to the play at Florida Studio Theatre on Wednesday night," she said. "And I promise you, I promise myself, I will come prepared for a long, long, long fun filled evening."

"I sure hope so. And a short, short play."

We walked to her Jeep and I gave her another hug and a kiss and watched her drive away. I missed her physically but didn't miss what was on her mind. Both would be on Wednesday night's agenda. Sugar always helped the medicine go down.

I turned to go back in the house and saw the moonlight reflecting off the front porch windows. When I remembered the sour look on Mangello's face, the moon went behind a cloud.

CHAPTER 5

The next morning my stomach ached as I paid bills; Florida Power & Light, AT&T, Comcast Cable, the sewer and water bill, car insurance and the credit cards. The good news was I had money to pay them. To handle the bad news I needed to get up and walk around the house. I needed to let off some steam. The bad news was I had $493 left in the bank. Unless one of the two deals I still had in the hopper closed soon, I'd be out of money before the end of next month. I needed what I had for food for Ethan. I wasn't letting him go hungry. It was years ago but I still remember what hunger felt like. Real hunger. It hurt. But for me, not as much as the shame, anger and confusion that came with it. No Ethan wasn't going to feel hunger, even if I have to …

I didn't forget to pay the mortgage payment. I knew I didn't have the money for that. If it weren't for Frank Mangello's willingness to work with me, this pressure cooker would have blown months ago. I decided if I ever have another son, I'd name him Frank.

It was only ten in the morning but seemed much later. I needed to relieve some tension. As always, Jim Beam was available for me in the cabinet. He was a patient guy but I headed to the garage instead.

I opened the garage door and there it dangled. The loyal and sacrificial Henry hung from the roof joist waiting for me to vent. I put on the red punching gloves and tore into it. Two left jabs, a right cross, another left jab. My angst started to lift. My mind cleared if only for a bit. I continued to rap the bag harder and harder.

***

Twenty minutes later the sweat poured off me. My shirt was soaked. Then I heard foot steps on the shell driveway. I looked out the garage door window. It was Frank Mangello. That wasn't good. One more hit, I slammed the bag as hard as I could and took the gloves off.

"Hello Frank. Two times I get to see you this week. I like that."

"Well I don't know how much you're going to like me today. I need to tell you something. And I see you've been hitting the bag, so promise me you won't hit me when I tell you."

"Don't worry about that Frank. Can I get you something to drink?"

"No thanks."

Mangello was skittish. I never saw him uptight. I put my hand on his shoulder and guided him to a chair.

"Please Frank, have a seat." Mangello plopped into the chair. "Tell me, what's going on."

"Not that I have to tell you but this economy is killing lots of people, figuratively if not literally. Sometimes I feel like I'm going to have a heart attack. And...and you know I'd do anything I could for you and Ethan"

"Frank you've been great to us. I'm grateful for how you've handled my current situation. I can't thank you enough."

Mangello surprised me when he sprang from his seat like a tight wire uncoiling, then stood behind the chair leaning on it for support.

"Things are not going easy for me right now," he said. "I've looked at every option but nothing works. I...I...I..."

"Frank, go easy and bottom line it."

He took a deep breath and spurted, "I need cash. I need to sell your mortgage and I need to do it quickly." He fell back down in the chair relieved. "I've been talking to three possible investors who are considering buying the paper from me and holding your mortgage. Of course, they won't give me the full amount, they'll discount it but it'll be enough for me to handle what I need to. Jake, I'm sorry but I need to do it as fast as possible."

I remained calm, at least outwardly, "So if I understand correctly, then I'll pay my mortgage payments to them instead of you. What about the past due payments?"

"That's the tricky part because I don't know how someone will deal with that, the payments will follow the paper. Let's hope they'll work with you."

I preferred to have Mangello hold the mortgage more than anyone. No one could have been any better for me. My sense was that this could only get worse.

"What sort of time frame are we talking about Frank? Do you know yet?"

"As it sits now, there are three parties interested and there's no telling how quickly this could go down. But I need money as soon as possible. I'm sorry Jake. I hope you understand."

I understood more than he could possibly know. This could get real dicey.

"Frank, I have two deals that could possibly close in this next month. Then I could not only catch up my payments and maybe even pay you in advance some money to get you out of your jam. Could that change your decision to sell my mortgage?"

"Jake, that's nice of you but the answer is no. A few payments are a drop in the bucket for what I need. I hold mortgages on twelve properties and half are late in payments. The others don't hold the equity I need. I hate to tell you this, but your property is the most valuable to me and the most saleable. You did a fantastic job of renovating it. It looks like a Bahamian jewel. And I remember you doing most of the work yourself. Believe me, your carpentry talents are legendary in this neighborhood."

My carpentry skills just bit me in the ass. I felt the teeth grab hold.

"Jake, I'm sorry but I've got to do this. I'm really sorry."

Anger pounded my head. I needed to hit Henry

even more.

"Frank, I'm sorry you're in this situation. I understand your dilemma and I wish I could help and not be part of the cause."

"You're not the problem Jake. You're just a victim of the bigger problem. Don't get me started about the banks."

I didn't want to get him started about the banks because I didn't want to get started about the damn banks.

"With this business out of the way, as much as it can be for now, can I get you something to drink?"

"Actually, I don't have time for a drink. I got a doctor's appointment. My chest feels like it's got a ten ton gorilla on it and I'm scared."

I knew the feeling. "I'm sure the docs going to tell you, it's stress and that you're strong as a horse. You just need a little stress reliever, the kind you put in the bank, the all in one green pill."

"That's so true. A nice green pill beats that little blue one right now," he said. Mangello laughed briefly but then immediately returned to being serious. "One more thing. These possible buyers may want to see the collateral, so you might have some strangers coming by to see the property. If they get serious, I'll need to arrange with you a time for them to see the inside."

"No problem. Thanks for the heads up."

Mangello got up and offered me his hand. We shook hands like two warriors against large forces, as indeed we were.

"Hope all goes well with the doc."

"Thanks."

After Mangello left, I sat for a few moments with my stomach turning and my head pounding. Rather than let my head get pounded, I chose to do the pounding. Back in the garage, the gloves went on again. I hit Henry with a right cross that made the 70 lb. bag jump back to the end of its three foot chain. When it came back, an upper cut sent it straight up in the air and when it came down a left cross knocked it clear off the chain and into the corner. Henry was done for the day.

CHAPTER 6

The last place I wanted to be was in a tight seat, in the first row of the Florida Studio Theatre waiting for the start of a play about a female band, stranded in a rickety saloon in the middle of nowhere Texas. On the other hand, the first place I wanted to be that night was right next to Camille wherever that might have been. The way I figured it, first I had to eat my vegetables before I got dessert.

As the theatre lights flickered on and off signaling the imminent start of the play, I saw a tall elderly, elegantly dressed man and a younger lady walking directly toward me. He was holding a glass of red wine filled to the rim. His eyes were fixed on the seats in the row directly behind me. Then for an instant, he looked me straight in the eyes and I recognized him. He was the old guy who talked with me after I dropped my coffee in Charlie's Newsstand.

"Won't spill a drop on you, unlike your coffee," he said in a gravelly voice.

"I have no worries about that. It looks like you have it totally under control." He remembered me.

"You don't have to worry about him," the woman said. "My father is as steady as a rock. Always has been, even after 90 years."

"90 years? No way," I blurted.

"As a matter of fact, 90 years old today. We're celebrating his birthday," she said proudly.

I held my hand out to shake his. He took my hand and shook it firmly. "Well happy birthday to you sir."

"Thank you."

The lights dimmed for the start of the play. I turned to Camille and whispered, "Can you believe that guy is 90?"

She poked my the leg and whispered, "The play is starting."

Seeing the old man reminded me about my lost Berk deal and my conversation with Mangello. My inner growl rose along with the curtain. A minute later, I thought of my two deals that hopefully would close this month. My body relaxed a bit and I did my best to get comfortable in the small seat.

The play was more a cabaret act than a story with a plot. I didn't recognize a single song. They must all have been written for this play. Can't say, I liked it but didn't hate it either. Camille was enjoying it, so that worked for me.

***

Forty-five long minutes later the curtain fell, intermission began and I was relieved. I gave Camille a hug. "This is a very unusual show. Quite amusing," I said.

"Jake Shaw I know you too well to buy that line but I thank you for your patience, and it's fun for me to have you here. In return maybe this season I'll go to a few Rays' games with you. Would you like that?"

"Only if you're not bored out of your mind."

"Maybe, I'll surprise you and finally learn some of the rules."

"Now that would be amazing. And…maybe I'll sing along with the songs after intermission."

She laughed, pinched my arm and kissed my cheek. "I'm going to the ladies room."

I stood to let her pass by me. I stretched a bit and then felt a tap on my shoulder. I turned around.

"Even with your lost deal, be thankful," the old man said.

He saw my confused look.

"She's a beautiful woman. Inside and out."

"Thank you sir. I totally agree with you." I hesitated. "Do you mind if I ask you a semi-personal question?"

He nodded his approval.

"How do you stay in such amazing shape? From the grip of your hand, you're as strong as an ox and you look as lean as a deer."

"Thanks," he said. Then his daughter chimed in.

"Nothing slows him down. His routine is full. When he first gets up in the morning he does yoga to lubricate the joints and stretch the fascia that got stiff through the night. Then he takes his walk for cardio. In the late afternoon he does a little more stretching and does some exercises with light dumbbells for the musculature. It sure works for him. Someday if you want to walk with him, you can find him every morning at 8:30 at the Bay Front Park right at the end of Ringling Blvd. But don't wear walking shoes. Wear running shoes. His walk is more like a run to me."

I looked at the birthday boy. "By the way, my name is Jake, Jake Shaw."

"Odin," he said.

"Excuse me?"

"Call me Odin."

"Nobody calls him by his real name. My father knows people from all over the world. They all just call him Odin. And I'm Sara."

I nodded and smiled at Sara but immediately returned to Odin. The theatre lights flickered interrupting our conversation.

"Nice to meet you Odin and Sara."

Camille returned to her seat as the theatre darkened. For the second half of the play, I sat mindless of what was happening on stage. I was thoroughly intrigued by the laconic old man behind me.

***

By the time I got home from taking Ethan's sitter to her apartment, it was 11 p.m. Without the slightest hesitation, I went directly to the bedroom. The room was lit with two bedside candles. Camille lay naked under the covers with one leg completely exposed. Odin was right. I was one lucky man, actually, the luckiest of men.

Her beauty called to me. As I took my off my

clothes, my eyes never left her. I slid into bed with her, into our private world. I wrapped my arms around her. She drew tightly into my chest. I lifted her face to me and softly kissed her moist bottom lip, then I slowly and gently covered her delicious mouth with mine. I pressed a little harder. She accepted. Then harder still. My body rose, I wanted to take her with the entire force of my being but I resisted. I've waited, we've waited, too long to rush our love.

CHAPTER 7

Robert Munroe was a class act. With thirty plus years as President and Owner of Munroe Realty Corporation, he had seen every type of situation and market imaginable. I'd never heard one unkind word about him from anyone. When he spoke, people listened, so the lack of attendance at that morning's sales meeting was totally indicative of the depressed real estate market. Nevertheless, Robert stood tall in the front of the meeting room, wearing a blue pin-striped suit, white shirt and red tie giving a pep talk and trying to rally his troops.

"The good news is that I believe we've hit the bottom of this market," Robert said to nine of us. "Hitting the bottom has always been an indicator for a new upward cycle. However in this market, the trouble is that we're not certain how long we'll be at the bottom. It could be a quick turn around but… my sense is we still have a few more months to go. The key to your survival and your success is to understand there are deals out there for the astute agent. This is a buyer's market and as soon as the buyers, investors, speculators think it's the bottom, they will venture out and you'll make money and plenty of it. Position yourself to take advantage of the situation. Be patience. Be smart. And most of all stay optimistic."

I had to give him credit. Robert Munroe was a man of optimism. I wanted to shake his hand and thank him for his pep talk. When he saw me approach him, he put out his hand to shake mine. He had a serious look on his face.

"Jake, do you have a minute. I was going to call you today, so can I talk with you in my office?"

"Sure. Now?"

"Yes, it's important. Please wait in my office and I'll meet you there in a few minutes"

"Deal," I said with a curiosity tinged with anxiety. Why would he want to talk with me? This had never happened before. I knew my production was non-existent but I wasn't alone in that category.

On his office walls were about thirty photographs of his career. There were pictures of him with a wide range of officials, dignitaries, politicians and celebrities. He had indeed been highly successful.

Five minutes later he entered his office and shut the door.

"Jake have a seat. Can I get you a coffee?"

"No thanks, I'm good."

He sat in the chair across from me.

"Jake, we've known each other for awhile. How long has it been?"

"Well, you're the only broker I've worked with in

my real estate career and that's going on twelve years."

"And I've watched you grow from a rookie to a real professional."

I felt his tension.

"Robert, you know me, just bottom line what you've got to say."

Munroe sat up straight, laughed and looked me right in the eyes. "You are indeed, a one of a kind guy."

"Robert?"

"Okay. Okay. Early this morning I talked with Dennis Muller over at Republic Bank. We talked about a number of matters including your Porter contract. It turns out that after Republic did its due diligence, Mr. Porter was not what he presented himself to be. To bottom line it Jake, your Porter deal is dead."

"No!" I blurted. I needed Henry.

"I'm afraid so."

"What happened?"

"Evidently, the bank found a number of defaulted loans Porter tried to bury. He's a smart operator, who's fooled more than a few institutions."

"Are they sure?"

"He's even operated under a number aliases. He's a pro, a real pro."

I shook. I stood up and walked around the room before I said something I'd regret. I fought the urge to pick up the paper-weight on Munroe's desk and throw it through the window.

"Jake, I'm sorry but this is the toughest market I've ever experienced. Personally I'd like to help you out and give you a draw but professionally I learned a long time ago to set a policy against giving draws and it's proven to be a good policy. However, what I am willing to do for the next year, starting right now, I'm going to change your commission split with the firm to 90-10. So you can keep 90% of the commission fees from any deal you do. This might give you some help."

The temperature of my blood could've boiled an egg. However, I summoned my respect and gratitude for Robert.

"I sincerely appreciate your offer. But I've still got to do a deal for anything to happen. And right now I have nothing but the Lorry deal in the hopper and that has maybe a fifty-fifty chance to actually happen."

Munroe stood up, walked toward me and extended his hand.

"All I can tell you is keep plugging away and it'll happen,"

"Thanks Robert, I know you mean it, so please convince my creditors of that."

***

Fifteen minutes later I turned the corner of my block and spotted a black Mercedes convertible parked right in front of my house. It looked familiar but I couldn't place it. As I approached it, the driver quickly pulled away. I assumed it was probably one of Mangello's investors checking the property. My jaw tightened when I thought of something happening to our home.

It was 11:05. With Ethan in school the house was empty except for my patient friend Jim Beam and I badly needed some of his company. The solid strength of the glass and the round shape of the bottle felt good in my hand. It had a heft to it that foretold of its substantial offering. I poured a shot. I took a moment and anticipated the taste it before it crossed my lips. My reflection in the microwave door looked back at me. I hesitated. This wasn't right and I knew it. I also knew where it could lead. Not now. Not ever again. I couldn't do it, so I dumped the booze down the kitchen sink and put the bottle back in cabinet.

I made myself a cup of coffee instead. The weather that April day was beautiful, so I went outside on the patio. I brushed the leaves off the lounger and dropped into it. I had a big decision to make and I needed clarity. I took a deep breath, closed my eyes and tried to relax but my skull was splitting. I envisioned being in a boxing ring getting punched by numerous invisible opponents. No matter how I maneuvered I was still getting hit. I couldn't see who to swing at and there was no way out of the ring. To make matters worse, Ethan was in the ring with me but so far I had kept them away from him. And I would be damned if I was going to let them get to him. He wasn't going to take any hits because of my ineptitude. That was for damn sure.

Sometimes the devil you knew was better than the devil you didn't know. Besides, I couldn't see any other options. I put down the coffee, went into the garage, grabbed the red gloves and started to take it out on Henry. After ten minutes, my decision was made. I had to do it.

The phone number was carved deep in my memory even though I hadn't dialed it for fifteen years. I tapped the numbers slowly. It rang a half-dozen times without any response. Maybe it was changed or disconnected. Part of me hoped that was the case but the other part of me needed it to work. Five more rings still no answer and there was no answering machine. Then just as I was going to hang-up, I heard an elderly woman answer.

"Hello? Hello? Who's there?"

I must have had the wrong number.

Then she said, "Don't be a wise guy. Say something or hang up. This is not a number to mess with."

I recognized the voice."Mrs. Villani?"

"Who's this?"

"It's Jake Shaw. Remember me? It's Jake."

"Jake? Is this you Jake? You sound like a man."

"I am a man now momma, at least I'm trying to be. And a father too!"

"I still see you like a boy eating my cookies."

"Save them for my son, Ethan. He'd love your cookies."

Momma Villani was always direct. Not much on small talk.

"You looking for Louis? He's not here. He's in Tampa."

"Tampa? As in Tampa, Florida?"

"Yes. You want his private cell number? This is the only number he answers."

"Thanks momma. Sure give it to me."

What's Louie doing in Tampa? Maybe he retired. Louie? Never.

I had another chance to re-consider this decision.

Did I really want to make this call? My life might never be the same again. Or Ethan's. Or Camille's. Well…it was just a phone call. I dialed the number.

A few rings and a gruff voice answered. "Who's calling me at this number?"

"Your mother gave me the number?"

"My mother? Don't play games with me. Who the fuck is this?"

"Louie, it's Jake. Jake Shaw."

"The Jake Shaw I knew died. Jake Shaw is dead."

My body tensed and I got aggressive. It felt like old times.

"Wait! Wait a second. I want say to something. I want to explain."

"Explain? Explaining ain't changing nothing."

"Listen Louie, I thought I'd explain over the phone but now we can do it face to face. Mano to mano." I challenged him. "Can you handle that?"

"Where the hell are you Jake fucking Shaw? You calling me from a cemetery?

"I'm in Sarasota."

"Sarasota? An hour south of here? That's a fucking long drive for a dead man."

"I've risen from the dead Louie. I've risen from the dead and I coming to see you."

CHAPTER 8

It was just after 9 in the morning, and the sun was still rising over Tampa Bay. The view of the bay from the top of the 430-foot high Skyway Bridge was spectacular. I checked my rear view mirror. It was rare but there was no traffic behind me, so I stopped on the peak of the bridge, got out of the car and walked to the railing. The beautiful panorama made me forget my problems. To the west, the historic pink landmark, the Don CeSar Hotel sat solid on the shore of the Gulf of Mexico. To the east was the city of Tampa shining in the rising sun. Beneath me and surrounding me was the aquamarine water of Tampa Bay. I wanted to stay on the bridge for as long as possible but with traffic approaching in the distance, I didn't want to press my luck. Besides I had to keep my appointment with Louis Villani.

Exactly forty minutes later in Tampa, I pulled into a palm tree lined parking lot for a Venetian, three story office building. There was no question of who owned the building. Prominently displayed across the roof's parapet was the sign, Villani Enterprises. Louie had come a long way from Brooklyn.

No expense was spared on the inside either. The sizeable lobby was styled with Italian marble on both walls and floor. Before I could take in the full view I heard my name called.

"Good morning Mr. Shaw. Mr. Villani will be with you shortly. Please have a seat. May I get you something to drink?" asked a stunning woman, probably her in late twenties.

I sat down on a black leather sofa. "No thank you. I'm good."

The magazines on the coffee table suggested money and plenty of it. I chose the current issue of Worth and began to thumb through it. Within a few minutes the elevator opened and an older, more sophisticated woman greeted me.

"Mr. Shaw, Mr. Villani is ready to see you now. Please follow me."

She led me into the marble elevator. We rose to the third floor, then we walked down a long hall, finally coming to a set of ten foot double mahogany doors. Without knocking she opened a door and entered, I followed. Behind a huge marble desk, dressed in an expensive grey suit was Mr. Louis Villani, looking more like Armani than Armani.

For a few moments, he looked like he'd seen a ghost. When he recovered, he nodded toward a large, ivory leather couch and pointed for me to sit. I complied. I sat and he stared at me from his desk across the room in taut silence for ten minutes before he spoke.

"What the fuck do ya want Jake Shaw? No let me guess. You're out of money and need a job. That's why you're here, isn't it?"

Before I could speak he held up his hand to stop me.

"Ya got balls. Ya really got balls coming here." He shook his head with disgust on his face. "I never thought I'd see your sorry ass again. And I really didn't give a shit. And right now, I still don't give a shit."

I sat up straight on the edge of the couch and leaned forward. "I can understand that."

"Ya don't understand shit. Ya don't understand what I felt like when ya left fifteen years ago. It felt worse then having my right arm ripped off. I was betrayed. Fucking betrayed. Ya hear me? Fucking betrayed. I treated ya like the kid brother I never had. And in this business, in this family business, betrayal could be punishable by death. So to me Jake Shaw ya died fifteen years ago. You're fucking dead."

His words were not easy to take. I could've gotten up and left and remained dead or do what I came there to do.

"Before anything else, I want to explain why I left. And this time you need to listen. It's important to the both of us, regardless of the reason I'm here."

He got up from his chair and moved to the front of the desk and leaned back on it. He smirked and folded his arms across his chest. "Go ahead dead man. Your time is short."

"Fifteen years ago I was going through some huge changes and I wanted to do what I thought was the right thing. I wanted what I never had, a normal family life and I found the woman I could do that with. Molly wanted the same thing and she deserved a normal man. And you know Louie, more than anybody, you know my life was anything but normal. On top of that, I was still young and I lacked experience and perspective. I made a choice that I thought was right for Molly and me."

"Did it turn out right for ya Jake? Did it? You're still, eh together?"

"She's dead Louie. Molly is dead."

Louie didn't say a word. He turned his head and looked out the window.

"Before Molly died she gave birth to a baby boy, my son. And I continued to do what I thought was right for him."

"So what's the difference now Jake? Don't ya still want to do what ya call right?"

I stood up and pensively walked to the window and saw my car in the parking lot. I thought of hauling kids to baseball games. Then I thought of not having food on the table for Ethan.

"In the past few years I found out there is no right or wrong. They, who made the rules, broke the rules. They, who had our trust to do the right thing, didn't. The trust we had in the banks and the government was shot to hell by their joint financial behavior. The banks proved to be as corrupt as organized crime, if not more so. And the government let them get away with it. They actually paid their bail. They gave them a get-out-of-jail card for free. And they did it with our money, while me and hundreds of thousands, if not millions of others, got crucified by doing the right thing and played by the rules. The thing I know now, the only right thing I know right now is to take care of myself and my family. There are no rules, there's no right thing.

"So ya went to the school of hard knocks. Why should I give a shit?"

"Because you're my family. The only one I've known and I didn't realize at the time."

"And ya ran out on your family fifteen years ago. We're back to square one Jake and your time is just about up."

As I slowly walked back to the couch acting remorseful, he got buzzed over his phone's speaker. His secretary announced, "Mr. V. your wife is on the line."

"Tell her I'll call her back in a few minutes. We're just about done here."

His wife? I had my next move.

"So Louie, you got married again. Man, I remember after you went through that horrible divorce with Lorraine you swore off marriage. Never, never, never, ever again you said."

His eyes twinkled, his face softened and he laughed. "Yeah, I never would've bet on it. We just had our first year anniversary… the best year of my life."

He picked up the frame on the desk, and brought it to me and proudly showed me her picture. "That's the Contessa." His grizzled demeanor faded.

"The Contessa?"

"Yeah, the Contessa. That's what I call her. That's what everybody calls her."

"Sounds like you found the one to make you happy Louie. Really happy."

"Yeah, for the first time in my life, I feel like God blessed me."

I leaned back on the couch and got comfortable.

"So if I understand correctly Mr. Villani, approximately seventeen years ago you were going through a hellacious divorce. And one year ago, you changed your mind and now you're the luckiest man in the world. I'll bet you're glad you gave marriage a second chance."

"Ya bet your ass on it, I am."

I moved to the edge of the couch, rested my elbows on my knees, tilted my head, put a smile on my face and looked him straight in the eyes. "Really now."

He saw my move. "Fuck ya Jake Shaw. It ain't happening."

I wasn't deterred. "Look at it his way. Another bet, says you learned a lot about yourself, other people and life. And because of it, you caught a break when the Contessa said yes to your proposal."

He put the picture back on his desk. He paused and took a deep breath. I knew I hit his soft spot. I sensed a small shift in him.

"What happened to the boy ya had with Molly?"

"His name is Ethan, He's ten and he's with me."

"What about him?" he asked.

"What do you mean, what about him?"

"This business is more complicated, faster, more hi-tech and riskier than ever before. We're into a lot of stuff now. One slip and your kid will be grown before you're out."

"I don't slip. You know that."

He hardened again. "No Jake, I knew that. I don't

know it now. I know nothing now. Remember you're dead to me. I'm having a conversation with a dead man."

"It seems we were both dead. You before the Contessa and now I'm trying to push away my tombstone."

Louie went back to his chair, sat down and pulled out a cigar but he just played with it in his hand. Again, we sat in an awkward silence for a few minutes.

"Louie, I have a question for you,"

"It's Mr. Villani or Mr. V. What's your question?"

"So Louie, what got you to Tampa?"

"I just told ya, it's Mr. V. And to answer your question, it's none of your fucking business. You're still one tough nut."

"So why not put me to work and I can help pay for those expensive cigars?"

He unwrapped the cigar, lit it, took a deep drag, held it and blew out the smoke.

"This is what I'm willing to do." A shorter drag, then came the blow. "Nothing… Nothing…Fucking nothing." He got up and walked to the window again and looked out at Tampa. Then he went back to his desk and sat. "But think about it. It's the best I can do, especially after a dead man walked into my office after all these years. You're fucking lucky I don't shoot you."

I walked over to the desk and handed him my card. "When will I hear from you?"

"Real estate eh? I was right. That's why you're here. The market sucks and you're broke."

"When can I hear from you?"

His face went cold and he glared at me. "Don't push. Or you'll really be dead."

I knew to give him room. "Gotcha."

"I told ya, the best I can do is think about. Understand?"

"I understand."

"Now get the hell out of here."

***

Fifty minutes after leaving Louie's office, I was driving south back to Sarasota, crossing the Skyway Bridge. Now there was no chance to stop and look around. If I did I'd be crushed by the parade of cars behind me. Going forward on the Villani highway however, could prove even more dangerous.

CHAPTER 9

"It's a good thing you're not playing baseball today dad. You'd drop every ball," Ethan said as he sat on the kitchen counter tossing a baseball in the air.

"No kidding." I bent down and picked up the second piece of bread I dropped on the floor making him French toast.

"My mind is in work mode this morning Ethan. There's a lot of stuff going on."

"I know what you mean dad."

I was impressed by my son's precociousness.

"You do?"

"Yeah, I gotta make a big decision."

"What're you deciding?"

"Which position to play, shortstop or third base."

Everything was indeed relative.

"Which one is more fun?"

He tossed the baseball in the air a couple of times. "I guess shortstop." He tossed the ball again. "Yeah shortstop, it's way more fun." He jumped down from the counter and plopped in his chair. "Wow, that's a load off my mind. Thanks dad."

"Glad I could help."

"Can I please have four pieces? And please, please, please not bread off the floor," he laughed.

I took the piece of dropped bread and gently threw it at him. He ducked and laughed at me. "You can't cook, you can't catch and you can't throw today either. Bad day eh dad?"

He had no idea. Much of the night, I thought of Louie and the world he lived in. It was a world that used to be as natural to me as breathing but then I had nothing to lose, except for time. With Ethan, was it worth the gamble? I knew that if something went wrong, his life would be changed forever. But I felt was out of choices.

When I finally did get a little sleep, I dreamt of the old man, Odin. In the dream he was a much younger man and he was about to tell me something, something really important, but I woke up before he could tell me. So after I dropped Ethan off at school, I played my hunch and drove to Bay Front Park to see if I could meet up with the old guy.

***

Bay Front Park was a great place to walk or run. Its half-mile looping path ran the perimeter of the seven acre park, right along the bay. At 8:40, I stood at the entrance to the park without a sign of Odin. I stretched a little on the bench and after a few minutes, I assumed he wasn't coming and decided to get a run in. The slight wind made ripples on the water and felt good on my face. I started slowly. About a quarter of the way, I lengthened my stride and picked up the pace. My legs felt strong so I continued the fast pace for the rest of the loop. When I reached the end, I saw Odin dressed in a blue warm up suit with a white baseball hat that matched his hair. I slowed down. He saw me and waved. As we drew near he nodded and smiled.

I bent over and caught my breath. "I've been waiting for you."

"I'm late this morning."

"Odin, do you mind if I walk with you?"

"Not at all. I'd like that."

We headed out on the north side of the loop around park, across from the marina. He did walk fast and he did it in silence. If there was going to be conversation I realized I needed to start it.

"You showed up in my dream last night."

"Is that so?"

"We were walking in this park, as we are now. However you were younger than you are right now."

"Sounds good to me."

"The dream was vague at best. We were talking and you were just about to tell me something, something really important and…and I woke up before you could tell me."

"So you want me to tell you now?"

"Wouldn't that be nice and easy?" I laughed. "It sounds ridiculous now that you say it, but in a sense, yes. I just followed my gut instinct, my intuition I guess and here I am."

"Always do that, always listen to your intuition."

"Right now I'll follow any leads that might help me get out of the mess I'm in."

"The mess?"

"Yes, my deal from the other day and all the other deals that went down the tubes. I haven't been able to close a deal in almost two years. I've been living off savings but now I'm down to my last nickel, so to speak. So when I had this dream I had to follow it up and see if you could help me. You know, that thing you said about learning on someone else's dollar. Maybe, just maybe, you really did have something to tell me, something that would shed some light on my situation that could make a difference."

"I see."

"Odin, haven't you ever felt like you were trapped in a large steel vice that kept closing tighter and tighter on you?"

"More than once."

"What did you do? How did you handle it? How'd you get out of it?"

"Jake, it seems to me, you're getting a wake up call."

"A wake up call? What's a wake up call?"

"The purpose of an alarm clock is to awaken you from sleep. Your financial mess is your personal alarm clock going off."

"What's it waking me up to?"

"Perhaps an entirely new way of being."

"A new way of being?"

"Yes."

"That sounds a bit ethereal. How is that going to help me in a real and practical way"

"It can effect everything in your life in the most practical way. It can enable you to take dominion over your life."

"Will it help get me out of my mess?"

"That's up to you."

"Will you teach me how to wake up, get me out of my mess and as you say, take dominion over my life?"

"No."

"No?"

"No."

"Then what's this shit about, learning on someone else's dollar?"

"Jake, I'm not your teacher. You're your own teacher. However, if we agree on the terms, what I'll do is share with you what I know from my own experience. What you do with it is up to you."

"What terms?"

"Listen with an open mind and do your homework?"

"Homework?"

"Inner work. Life is an inside out game."

"Odin, I am sincerely working as hard as I can, doing whatever I can to solve and get through this situation. The market is horrible. I just don't understand what you're talking about."

"Do your homework. You will."

"I don't have a lot of time. The clock is ticking on my financial time bomb. I need to wake up and disconnect the wires before it goes off and totally ruins my life, as I know it. Can doing some homework really benefit me? And how long is this going to take?"

"For both questions, same answer, it's up to you."

"Did it work for you?'

"It did. Still does."

"Okay, I'm game. I'm ready to do anything that will help. When can we start?"

"Next time."

"When is next time? Wait! I know…it's up to me."

"Exactly."

The rest of our walk was done in silence. We simply nodded to each other at the end. Homework?

CHAPTER 10

As Camille and I pulled into my driveway the dashboard clock changed to 10 p.m. We were coming from seeing a foreign film at Burns Court Cinema. It was a long, slow movie and highly moralistic. Not exactly what I needed, considering the possibility of working with Louie again. I dozed off a few times during the film, thankfully. Also thankfully, I didn't snore.

I turned the ignition off and we sat in silence for a moment. Then Camille leaned over and rubbed my arm. "How about when we get inside I pour myself a glass of Pinot and pour a tall bourbon for you? How does that sound?"

"Perfect."

It was Saturday night, I was with the love of my life, a beautiful, intelligent, compassionate woman and all I wanted to do was disappear or grapple with Henry.

In the kitchen, she handed me the bourbon and said, "It's a beautiful night. How about we go outside, sit under the stars and count our blessings?"

She was right about the night. The temperature was 72 degrees, with a slight breeze. The sky was crystal clear with millions of twinkling stars.

Camille sat on the lounge. "Come over here and snuggle up with me," she said.

Usually I derived tons of pleasure from being close to her. That night I was numb to everything. Even the taste of the bourbon was flat like stale beer. I physically complied with her request and snuggled up to her but mentally I was millions of miles away and she knew it.

"Jake where are you tonight?"

"What do you mean, where am I tonight? I'm right here with you."

"Here with me is the last place you are. You might be on Jupiter for all I know. Come back to earth Jake. Be with me. Can you do that?"

I moved in closer to her, wrapped my arms around her and gently squeezed her.

"That's better. Your body made it back, now where's the rest of you, your mind, emotions? I need all of you. I miss you."

I took a sip of bourbon, and gave her another gentle squeeze. Jupiter didn't seem like a bad place to be at that moment. I smiled at her and kissed her cheek but my silence continued. We sat quietly for a heavy few minutes but I didn't fool her.

"Jake, either you're not hearing a word I'm saying or you don't care. Which is it?"

"It's neither Camille. It's just that…"

"It's what Jake? What?"

"Nothing…it's nothing."

"Then why are you so withdrawn from me? And it's

just not tonight. This past week, you've been in your own world, a world that doesn't allow me in. Please Jake talk to me. What's going on?"

I swallowed the rest of the bourbon.

"I'm going to get another drink. Do you need some more wine?"

"Jake, what I need is for you to be with me, actually be present with me. Will you do that when you come back?"

"Need more wine?"

"No Jake, I don't." She sighed. "Jake, I told you what I need."

I smiled at her and nodded my head. She took a deep breath and sat back on the lounger with a puzzled look on her face. I went into the kitchen and poured a full the glass with bourbon, no ice. I hesitated to go back outside. There was no way I was going to tell her I'm about down to my last nickel and I might go back to work for a small time gangster, who doesn't seem so small time anymore. There was no upside to that. I didn't want her to worry but I also didn't want her to think less of me. My head was spinning but not from the alcohol. I thought maybe if I waited, my situation would all clear up by itself. That was magical thinking at its best.

I stepped on to the patio and saw her standing, glaring at me. I knew the look. It had been awhile since I last saw it. It was back when we first started hanging out together. I thought it was a thing of the past. It was far from pretty.

"Camille, please don't go there. Please. There's no need to do this. Not now. Not again. Please."

She didn't hear a word I said. I tried to put my arms around her but she pulled away. She slugged down her wine and headed inside. I knew to let her go. Through the kitchen window I saw her pour another glass of wine and down it. When I saw her eyes fill up with painful tears, I went inside.

"Camille, this is not what you're thinking. It's not. Please trust me. Trust my love for you."

"You know Jake, I've heard those words before. I trusted those words before and they were hollow. Hollow. You're right Jake. Not again. I don't deserve it."

"You're right Camille. You don't deserve it and…"

"And what Jake? What? What?"

I took a deep breath. "I don't deserve it either. I'm not him."

"You're all alike. No difference. No difference at all."

She grabbed her purse off the counter and stormed for the door.

"Camille. Please Camille don't go. Please don't go."

The front door slammed. It was useless to go after her. I heard her get in her car, start the ignition and peel away.

From experience I knew there was nothing I could do for her tonight. I was alone with a life I wanted to kick the shit out of. I downed the full glass of bourbon, grabbed the bottle, left my glass on the counter and went back outside. I sat in the lounge chair, now without Camille. I was alone with Jim Beam.

I was glad Ethan was spending the night with Matthew. He loved Camille and this would have upset him. Hell, even though I was on Jupiter, this still upset me. My mind whirled like a cyclone as my heart sank like a torpedoed submarine. The good news was the bourbon started to taste better.

CHAPTER 11

The night dragged me into the dawn. I knew I couldn't come clean with Camille about what I might be doing. That wouldn't work on a number of levels. But then again, I realized deep in my heart, I didn't want to lose her. I was stuck. I decided to run on the beach hoping to get the clarity I needed.

It was a few minutes before sunrise and the beach was empty except for a few ambitious shell seekers and tribes of seagulls and sandpipers scurrying around the shore looking for their morning meal. That's how I preferred the beach, empty. It gave me the space to collect my thoughts and feelings without distractions.

Siesta Key beach is an excellent beach to run on. The crunch of the damp crystal sand beneath my feet always felt good. In the dim light of sunrise I focused on the blue lifeguard station about a quarter mile down the beach. I started to jog. My legs were strong and my breathing was easy. After a hundred yards I broke into a full sprint toward the station. I dug inside me and released the tension. I ran passed a couple of people along the shore and then through the birds, scattering them. It felt so exhilarating when I got to the blue station I blew right by it and headed for the yellow station, another hundred yards farther down the beach. As I approached the yellow station, I saw a woman waving. Getting closer to her I realized she was waving at me. It was Camille. I slowed down and walked to her. She was smiling and that felt even more exhilarating than running ever could. Her arms were open waiting for me to enter her embrace. I gladly glided right into her.

"I'm sweaty," I warned.

"I couldn't care less," she said.

We held our embrace as the tide rushed around my feet soaking my running shoes but there was no way I was letting go.

She sighed in my ear, "I'm sorry."

I separated just a little. "For what?"

"For my lack of patience last night. For leaving. For hurting you with something that had nothing to do with you. I honestly thought I was done with that."

I pulled her closer to me, resting her chest on mine and her head on my shoulder. "I love you Camille. I really do love you."

She squeezed into me as close as possible. "I know."

"Camille, I know I've been withdrawn and quiet. I have plenty on my mind but it has nothing to do with you or us."

"Listen, I just got scared last night. I have never felt this way about anyone before you. And I just got spooked. I trust you Jake, more than I have ever trusted anyone. And last night that trust just wobbled and it won't happen again. You process what you need to process in your own way, in your own time. You'll tell me what you want, when you want it and how you want it. That's who I'm going to be for you."

I took a deep breath of relief. She was indeed an amazing woman. We walked in silence holding hands to the end of the beach where we parked our cars.

"Will I see you and Ethan later?" she asked.

"Ethan comes home around noon from Matthew's house. How about we have a Sunday brunch in the backyard?"

"That sounds great. I'll be at your house by noon."

We hugged each other, holding our hearts close.

"Jake, I feel closer to you now than ever. Thank you."

I kissed her gently on her lips. "And I, thank you."

***

A half hour later, I was just about to hop in the shower and my phone rang. I didn't recognize the number.

"Hello. This is Jake Shaw."

"Hi Jake. This is Paul Langrock. Sorry to bother you on a Sunday morning but I need your help."

Why did the most successful realtor at Munroe Realty need my help?

"What can I do for you Paul?"

"Jake, I have this $7,200,000 listing on Long Boat Key please sell it for me."

"Done. Now what else can I do for you?" I joked.

"Actually, here's the deal. I do have this $7,200,000 listing on Long Boat Key and I have scheduled a catered open house for it today. I arranged for a nice spread of munchies for the people who show up for it. And to enhance that possibility, I've taken a sizeable ad in today's open house section of the newspaper."

"Sounds like you have it under control, so what can I do?"

"Here's the thing. I've got a family emergency that needs my attention, so I asked Robert who'd he suggest for someone to work the open house for me and without hesitation recommended you. So are you up for it?"

"Paul it certainly sounds inviting but I need to make sure I can arrange some things before I tell you yes. Can I call you back in about 10 minutes?"

"Sure thing but please call back as quickly as possible, I need to solidify this situation. And Jake, here's some added incentive. I've been working with few prospects on the deal, they're seriously interested but so far haven't committed. All of them are aware of the open house today, if one of them shows up and you put them on contract, I'll gladly turn them over to you, so you'll get the selling side of the commission and I'll give you 25% of the listing commission too. So you have the potential to make yourself a nice piece of change today. So let me know if you can do it. Okay?"

"I'll be back to you shortly Paul," I said calmly. "And thanks for calling me."

This was the break that could turn my life around. Ethan? I had promised him we'd hang out together. I also needed to call Camille.

"Hi darling. Change of plans."

"What's up?" she asked.

"I just was asked to sit an open house today for an in-house listing selling for over $7 million.

"Jake, that's terrific. I'm so excited for you. If you need me to watch Ethan, I'd love to spend the day with him."

"Thanks for offering but I thought, he might get a kick out of hanging out there with me."

"Jake this is exciting. I'm rooting for you."

"There's even more to it than I can tell you now but I'll tell you when I see you and I'm holding a signed contract. How's that for confidence?"

"That's my man. You go for it."

***

At 12:30 Ethan and I arrived at a magnificent three story white structure, sitting on what looked like an acre of land right on the Gulf of Mexico. The architecture was so decidedly Grecian that as we drove up the driveway, it gave me the feeling that we were on the Greek island of Mykonos rather than Long Boat Key, Florida. Inside I found one surprise after another. From the front door there was a direct view of the crystal clear gulf waters. The living room extended two stories high with a wall of light azure glass and sliding glass doors, which faced the water and opened directly onto the beach. The great room could fit the Sarasota Symphony Orchestra and the kitchen, with multiple ovens, sinks and appliances, could feed them without a problem. The theatre room had two-dozen ultra-posh theatre seats. Each of the six bedrooms had it's own on-suite bathroom and Jacuzzi tub. All had king size beds. No expense was spared in the construction. But what captured Ethan's attention the most was the palm tree shaped swimming pool.

"I see where I'm going to be spending the day. Can I jump in now dad?"

It was a good thing his shorts could double as a bathing suit and there were towels in the SUV.

"I see no reason why not?"

"Hey dad, how come we don't have a house like this?"

He asked an obvious question with complete innocence but I pretended not to hear him.

"How come dad?"

"How come what?"

"That we don't live in a house like this?"

My ego and competitive pride was taking a licking. "Cause I don't make enough money."

"How come? Don't you want to?"

Ouch! The front door bell rang. Saved by the bell.

"I've got to see who's at the door. Enjoy the pool."

My pulse quickened as I opened the door, hoping it was a hot prospect but it was the caterer with a spread equal to the house. I showed him to the kitchen. He started to lay out the goodies and I asked him, "What happens if there is food left over?"

He continued to prep the food and without looking up answered me. "Mr. Langrock instructed me to tell you that it's yours and you should take it home and enjoy it. Thanks for reminding me to tell you."

"It'll take us a week to eat all this food," I said.

He didn't say a word. He was totally focused on preparing the food.

***

Three hours later without even a gecko showing up, no less a buyer, my enthusiasm was withering. What about the great ad? Where are those hot prospects? I nibbled on a few shrimp and went back out to be with Ethan.

"How you doing? You turning into a fish?'

"Dad, this is a really cool place. How often can we do an open house here?"

"Not a bad question Ethan. Not a bad question. I don't really know."

"Find out, will you? This is cool."

Just as I got comfortable in a pool chair I heard a voice coming from inside the house. Can this be one of Langrock's potential buyers? I went in to find out.

I found middle-aged couple standing in the living room. They looked well heeled. I sensed they've been here before. The man ignored me but the woman asked, "Is Paul Langrock here today?"

"No. Paul isn't here today. He had a family emergency to deal with. I'm Jake Shaw. He asked me to sit in for him. How can I help you?"

When the man heard Paul wasn't there, he walked away into the great room. The lady engaged me.

"My husband and I had hoped to talk with Paul today. We have a few questions, sort of negotiating points. We've been here a number of times and overall like the house but we'd prefer to make some changes and we're hoping to talk with Paul."

"Maybe I can help with those questions."

"No I don't think so. No offense to you Mr..."

"Shaw. Jake Shaw."

"No offense to you Mr. Shaw but with the asking price on this house of $7, 200,000, we'd like to talk with someone who can make some decisions. Besides...," she nodded toward her husband in the great room and whispered, "He doesn't want the house. I do. He's doing it for me. And he better, if he knows what's good for him."

"I understand. Is there anything I can show you while you're here? Maybe to help him like it more."

"Mr. Shaw..."

"It's Jake. Call me Jake."

"Jake, to be honest, it's not so much the house. He'd rather be in California closer to his kids. But my mother's here, so that's the way it's going to be. At least for a while."

"Well then, can I offer you some of this nice food?"

"Thanks but we just finished lunch at the Long Boat Key Club. Please tell Paul I hope everything works well for his family and we'll be in touch with him." She walked into the great room, pulled her husband's arm and out they walked.

The visit was quick, unprofitable and deflating. I went back out to the pool to see how Ethan was doing?

"Did you sell it, dad? Did you?"

"Not even close little buddy. It was like getting ready for your game and by the time you get to the field, the rain is coming down in buckets and the game gets called off."

"Bummer."

"The good news is that with all this food we are going to have ourselves a party tonight. So get your body out of the pool, and get dried off while I pack up the food. We're going home in about fifteen minutes."

I would've liked to have written a nice fat contract but just being in that house, with such an abundant environment, juiced me up a bit. My hope was maybe something else would come out of the blue and change things. I was ready for it. Big time.

CHAPTER 12

Once again I had a dream where Odin was talking to me. This time, we were standing in the great room of the huge house on Long Boat Key. But like the first time I dreamt of Odin, when I woke up, I didn't remember what he was saying. After dropping Ethan off at school, I headed to Bay Front Park

At 8:30, I was finishing a slow run around the loop when I spotted Odin at the entrance. He saw me and nodded. I quickly caught up with him and we began to walk in stride. After ten minutes of walking in silence, I cleared my throat and broke the silence.

"I'm anxious to answer my wake up call Odin. So what's on today's agenda?"

In a low voice he said, "The universe."

I laughed. "Might as well start small and work our way to bigger things. But seriously Odin, what are we going to talk about today?"

He turned his head, looked at me and grinned, "The universe."

My gut sank. "No offense, but how the hell is that going to help me?"

He spoke a little louder. "Jake what I have to tell you, which might help you with your situation, is not like popping a pill and it's all better. It's a process, a process that will require your participation and your patience. Should I continue or not?"

"Fair enough. Didn't mean to get testy. I just want to get out of this vice I live in. Yes the universe, please continue."

We walked a quarter of the loop in silence. I wondered if making me wait was my first lesson in patience. A moment later he spoke.

"It's huge, the universe is absolutely enormous. It's so beyond our normal comprehension that we don't give it much thought but we really should because it would give us a perspective that we sincerely need and could benefit from. Succinctly, my suggestion to you is to invest some time and get to appreciate the universe we live in."

I took a deep breadth and found a modicum of patience.

"Do you mean learn about the universe? Like in researching it, collecting a bunch of facts and information?"

"Information and facts are certainly helpful but they're not the whole picture and only part of what I'm suggesting."

"What do you mean?"

"Facts and information are flat, lifeless and can be less than inspiring. Just knowing information is not experiencing it. For example, knowing the aeronautics and mechanics of how an airplane flies is not the same experience as flying it solo."

"No doubt."

"Here's some information, some facts. The galaxy we call home, the Milky Way, is only one of 170 billion observable galaxies. Only one of 170 billion! Think about the enormity of it. And that beautiful Sun, rising over those condominiums, is 93 million miles from the ground we're walking on. Or that the planet we're walking on, has a circumference of 24,901 miles and a weight of 5.9 thousand trillion metric tons. And consider that Earth, has been floating in perfect orbital order, for the last 4.5 billion years. Which is still 9.2 billion younger than the rest of the universe. Got that?"

"Not really."

"Exactly. So in your quiet time, I suggest you try something like this. Do your own research and gather information that strikes a cord with you. There is plenty of it on the internet and in books. Google it, look on Youtube. The Hayden Planetarium has a good website to check out. But just don't write the information down or try to memorize it but rather have fun with it. Imagine yourself flying around in space visiting stars and planets. For example, an easy trip would be to the moon. There are plenty of pictures to stimulate your imagination. Allow yourself to feel the awesomeness, the enormity of the universe. Let your imagination take you beyond normal thinking. Call it whatever you want, meditating, contemplating or even surfing the universe. Whatever, wherever draws you, go for a ride in space. The main thing is to begin to develop an awareness of what's out there beyond your daily life."

My impatience was raging through my body.

"Odin, again I mean no disrespect, but all this seems a bit way out there and truly impractical. I see no earthly way this is going to help me. How is this going to help me?

"Think of what I suggest as a simple and potentially fun homework assignment. Homework is good for you and it's necessary to the process. And remember this is a process."

"But you didn't answer my question. How is this going to help me?"

"Are you going to do your homework or not?"

"If you answer my question."

"Perhaps in time your own experience will give you the answer to your question. But that Jake, depends entirely on you."

I took a deep breath trying to cool my blood down.

"As we come to the end of the loop, do you have anything else you want to tell me?" I asked hopefully.

"No," he said flatly, as he walked out of the park.

My frustration was over the moon. I needed to run long and hard. I headed over the Ringling Bridge about a mile from the park. I sprinted to the bridge and then back and forth over the half-mile expanse a half a dozen times. My frustration stayed with me for the whole run, like a dog barking and nipping at my heels.

***

At 6 p.m. I stood at the front door waiting for Ethan to put on his baseball shoes.

"If you don't get into gear it's going to get dark before we get there and there'll be no baseball tonight."

He flew around the corner. "I'm ready. I'm ready. Let's go. What are you waiting for?"

"I'm waiting for you funny boy. You forgot your bat!"

As we pulled away from the driveway, I saw in my rearview mirror a black Mercedes convertible roll up to the front of our house and stop. My stomach sank. I wanted to go back and check it out.

"Come on Dad, drive faster. Now who's the slow poke?"

I turned to Ethan and saw his magical smile. "Good call buddy."

I wrestled with worry for a few seconds and then forced it out of my mind, determined to be fully present with my son and give him quality time.

After a quick ride, we arrived at the baseball field. We were in luck, there was no one there; we had the entire field to ourselves.

"Dad I want to play shortstop great this year and I need practice fielding. Will you hit me some grounders?"

"You got it."

I hit him a slow one. He scooped it right up. I hit one a little faster. He scooped it up easily.

"Hit them harder. Those were too easy," he said.

I hit the next one harder than I thought I should, but he scooped that one up too. He was like a vacuum cleaner sucking up ground balls.

"Ethan you're doing great. You'll be the best shortstop in the league."

I increased the velocity and he began to miss some of them. I dropped back and lessened the force. Slowly I increased the speed and the human vacuum cleaner did his thing. After thirty minutes, he seemed a little tired.

"Hey Derek Jeter, need a break? How about some water?"

"Water please."

I handed him a bottle of water. He downed it with one swig.

"I need to get better on the really hard ones."

"Ethan, you are doing well. Some of the harder ones I hit you, even Jeter himself, would have had trouble handling. Pretty soon the Yankees will be wanting you to play for them."

"Dad, come on. You gotta be really good to play for the Yankees."

"So, you'll be real good."

He took another bottle of water and sat on the grass. I sat down next to him.

"How good were you Dad?"

I sighed and felt regret.

"Ethan, the truth is I was really good. I was a pitcher."

"Then how come you didn't play for the Yankees?"

"When I was growing up I needed to work to help your grandmother with the bills. So I didn't get to practice as much as I needed. Nevertheless, I was still the best pitcher in my high school division. We were expected to win the championship because I was pitching and I was un-hittable. There were about a dozen scouts from major league teams in the stands to see me pitch the championship game."

"Wow! You were really good. What happened?"

"It was a close game, score was 1-0 in our favor. It was the ninth inning I was pitching. Two outs. Two strikes on the batter. If I get the batter out, we win the championship. And with all the scouts there I was sure to get signed by a major league team. I threw a fast ball. The kid hit a fly ball down the left field line. As the left fielder was running to catch the ball, his ankle twisted and he fell down and he missed the ball. By the time he got up and threw the ball to the infield, the batter had reached third base. I was of course, disappointed but also determined to get the next batter to strike out and not to let the runner score, so we could win."

"Did you? Did you strike him out?"

"The first two pitches I threw were fast balls. Straight and fast. The batter swung at both and missed. Two strikes. The catcher called for the next pitch to be a curve ball to fool the batter. I didn't want to throw a curve, something about it just didn't feel right to me. I wanted to throw another fastball. But the catcher was smart and usually right. So I threw the batter a curve ball."

"What happened?"

"As I threw the ball, I heard my shoulder pop and then I felt the pain. I tore my rotator cuff and ligaments in my shoulder. It was never the same. Back then the doctors didn't know how to fix it, so my career was over with one pitch."

Ethan looked shocked. He didn't know what to say but his sad face said it all.

"That's why I'm glad you want to play shortstop. That doesn't happen to shortstops. And you get to play everyday. Pitchers play only when they pitch and that doesn't happen every game."

"And shortstops get to hit too. I like to hit a lot. Will you pitch some to me, so I can get some batting practice?" He hesitated. "That's if it doesn't hurt your shoulder."

"No son, that wouldn't hurt my shoulder. Not at all. In fact, it'll make my shoulder happy."

***

7:30 p.m. I turned the corner on to our street and thought of the black Mercedes and remembered when I first saw that same car. It was by Ethan's school on that rainy morning. My gut wrenched and I in turn wrenched the stirring wheel. What the hell was that guy doing in front of my house?

CHAPTER 13

The Sarasota Board of Realtors meeting room was ice cold. It was the regular monthly, early morning, sales meeting. Some local banker was telling a group of realtors the state of the economy, as if the struggling realtors didn't know it already. I liked to sit in the back of the large room where I could observe the entire situation. The size of the crowd had dwindled considerably over the past couple of years because of the lack of good news in the market. A large number of agents had left the business while others still somewhat in the business were hiding under rocks. I tried to attend these meetings regularly. I figured if I could pick up one small piece of information that helped me put bread on the table, my time was well invested. Today however, was not one of those days. The speaker wasn't saying anything of interest or telling us how to thread the needle and make some money. I listened with one ear.

With the other ear I listened to myself and came

to terms with what I had to do. It had become crystal clear. I knew I needed to go see Louie Villani again. I didn't want to but I desperately needed to. I made good money with Louie in New York back in the day. Granted that was fifteen years ago, which in that business, could just as well have been a century ago. There was no telling what he was up to in Tampa. I assumed it could be a lot worse. Nevertheless, I had to find out.

When the banker finished talking, a different speaker tried his best to raise the confidence of the dogged agents left in the room. The trouble was he didn't believe the words coming out of his mouth. He was like a cheerleader still doing cheers while his team was getting trounced. I gave him credit for trying but I couldn't wait around for the finale. I bolted through the backdoor to escape the depressed energy and headed to meet Blackie at Moe's Place.

***

The crowd at Moe's Place was still going strong. But there was no sign of Blackie, which surprised me. He was always early. His usual table was empty so I grabbed it. The waitress remembered me and nodded her approval, canceling any evil eyes coming in my direction. I picked up a loose newspaper, ordered a decaf and waited.

Fifteen minutes later, Blackie walked through the door with a big smile on his face. He headed straight toward me.

"Hey, I'm sorry I'm late. I hate it when I'm late.

But got some good news." A half-minute after he sat down, the waitress showed up with his black coffee.

"What's the good news?"

"My partner for ten years on the force, Marty Fitzsimons, he was a great partner, loyal, tough, smart, always had my back, always." He took a swig of coffee. "You'd like him. Actually you kind of remind me of him, a little."

Then he paused and stared out the window, with a haze over his eyes, like he was back in some scene in the past.

"And the good news?"

"What? What?"

"What's the good news?"

"Oh…Marty called me. His latest surgery went well. His fourth and hopefully the last."

"Why did he need so many surgeries?"

He winced, bit his lip and took a deep breath. "One night we were off duty, having a few beers in a local hangout. I went to take a leak. When I was in the bathroom, I heard a shot. I ran out and saw a guy bolting through the door. Then I looked over and saw Marty on the floor in a pool of blood."

"What the hell happened?"

"An argument broke out between two drunk hoods. They shoved each other, normal stuff. Then one guy punched the other guy, and the guy who got hit pulled a gun out. Marty stood up, pulled his weapon, showed his badge and told the guy to drop the gun. Somebody behind the bar dropped a glass, which distracted Marty for just an instant. The hood panicked and shot Marty in the gut and ran out the door. I saw the shooter running out but my instinct was to take care of Marty."

Blackie grimaced and took another drink of his coffee.

"He was hit bad. The bullet hit multiple organs. He was bleeding heavily. We rushed him to the hospital and he was in intensive care for a long time. It's a good thing Marty was built like a tank. A real good thing."

"What about the shooter? Was he caught and put away?"

Blackie looked for the waitress, like he was done with the conversation.

"Well was he?"

"No."

"What do you mean? Didn't witnesses see this guy? Someone had to know him? What about the guy who punched him? He had to know him. You must feel horrible that he didn't get caught."

Blackie's face hardened. "What I feel horrible about was that I wasn't there to protect my partner. And... I didn't say he didn't get caught. He just disappeared."

"What do you mean disappeared? Didn't you find him?"

"Disappeared. End of story."

At that moment the waitress came to the table with a pot of coffee and took our orders. Blackie ordered and then hustled to the bathroom. My phone rang. It was Frank Mangello.

"Hello Frank. What's up?"

"Jake, I want to keep you current on what's happening with your mortgage."

"And, what's that?"

"Well for me, there's good news. I still have three possible prospects. Two are solid with the third being especially strong and aggressive."

"Aggressive?"

"Yeah, like he's hyper-fixated on doing the deal. When I told him I had two other prospects he demanded to know who they were and how much they were offering. He just seemed a bit off, if you know what I mean."

"Any chance he drives a black Mercedes convertible?"

"As a matter of fact he does. How'd you know? Anyway I thought I'd let you know."

"Thanks Frank. I appreciate it."

Blackie came back to the table. He squinted at me. "What's up? That look on your face tells me there's trouble."

I bit into my bagel and sipped some decaf.

"So there's never been a word on the shooter? He just disappeared?" I asked again.

He looked down at his plate, filled his fork and said, "Like I said. End of story." Then he bit into a piece of bacon and I dropped the conversation.

CHAPTER 14

"Good morning Mr. Shaw. How are you this morning? Is Mr. Villani expecting you?"

"No, not this morning Ms. Roma. Not this morning. I thought I'd surprise him."

Her charming toned changed quickly. "Mr. Villani doesn't like surprises. I'm sure he won't see you without an appointment. It's best if you to call his assistant, Mrs. Martini and set up an ---." She turned her head abruptly toward the lobby door. "Good morning Mr. Villani."

I smiled at Louie. "Good morning Mr. Villani."

"Jake, what are ya doing here? It's… good to see ya again. Please, please come to my office."

I gave Ms. Romo a wink and a smile.

When we got to Louie's office he offered me some coffee.

"Decaf if you've got it."

He buzzed Mrs. Martini, "Two coffees. Make one a decaf."

He pointed to the sofa. "Sit there."

I plopped into the leather sofa.

"What the hell are ya doing here, Jake?"

"What I'm doing here is this. You said you would think about us having a new arrangement. Today I came to hear what your thinking."

He was caught off guard, recoiled and then recovered.

"I haven't given it a fucking thought. Been too busy."

" Sounds to me like you can use some help. And I know just the guy to help you."

His face flushed.

"Jake your visit surprised me and I don't like surprises."

"So I heard."

"I thought the last time I gave you enough of a clue that it ain't gonna happen. Now I'm telling ya straight, it aint gonna happen. Is that clear enough for ya? Do ya hear me?"

"Louie, you of all people, you're the one who taught me to never hear what I don't want to hear. I can't hear a word you're saying. Is that clear?"

"Ya still got guts Jake. I gotta give ya that. But my thinking is still the same. I ain't taking the risk."

"Risk? What risk? Me? You've got to be kidding." I brushed the hair on my head. "The only thing I ever did to upset you was to go clean. Never once, not ever did I ever do anything that put you in jeopardy. What risk you talking about?"

"Here's the risk. I'm not alone anymore. I have partners. And they're demanding. They don't like imperfections."

"Listen, I know I have stuff to learn and you know I learn fast."

He checked his watch. "I gotta a meeting to go to. I don't know why I'm doing this but if ya want to keep talking, you've gotta take a little ride with me."

"Let's go."

Fifteen minutes later we pulled onto to the lot of Villani Encore Motors. Seven beautiful exotic cars were sitting front row center on the lot. Behind them were Mercedes, BMWs, Jaguars, Porsches. About twenty in all. A prefab office building sat in the back of the lot, with an anxious looking guy standing on the front steps. He looked like he'd been knocked around a New York block a few times. As we got closer to him, I saw the sweat on his brow.

"Jake, this is Nick. Nick is the manager of this enterprise. He and I have some business to discuss."

We entered the building and Louie and Nick went into a back room. I stayed in the front. I leafed through a copy of the Dupont Registry, a magazine of fine and exotic cars. Minutes later, I heard arguing in the back room. Louie was irritated. The guy sounded scared but held his ground. A cell phone rang. Louie came out of the office, walked out the door onto the lot. A half-minute later Nick showed his face.

"You work for these guys?" Nick asked.

I shook my head, gave him a trusting look and nodded him on.

"These jerks want to take a key man life insurance policy out on me for a quarter million dollars. They say I'm the key to this business being profitable. Hell, as soon the policy becomes valid, the profit they'd make would be from whacking me for that a quarter of a mil. The hell with that shit. If you're not involved with these assholes, don't do it. No matter what they promise you. I'm getting out as soon as I get my next paycheck."

A minute later Louie came back in the office, a lot calmer than he left. He looked at Nick.

"Nick, I gotta go now. Think about what I said. It's to your benefit. I'll get back to ya later in the week."

Nick didn't say a word. He wanted his paycheck.

In the car Louie said, "I need to eat. I'm starving. Ya hungry?"

"I could use some food."

"Good let's eat."

Five minutes later, we pulled into a parking spot of new strip center with the Sunrise Café on the corner. It was a breakfast and lunch joint that looked crisp, clean and empty. The cashier, the waiters, the cook, addressed Mr. Villani like he was the king. He headed directly to what appeared to be his throne.

Immediately a beautiful waitress came over with black coffee for Louie and took my order. She gave a flirty smile to Mr. Villani. He smiled back. Five minutes later she came back with an omelet for me, and two eggs sunny side up with two slices of crisp bacon for Mr. Villani.

"Is everything to your satisfaction Mr. Villani?' She asked respectfully.

"Yeah, it looks clean. Thanks."

As I prepared my omelet Louie inhaled his food like a train going through a tunnel. A minute later, the waitress cleared his plate and poured him more coffee.

"So Jake, let's get down to brass tacks."

I quickly swallowed the food that I was chewing and came out aggressive.

"The tacks are these. I want back in. I need to do it."

"Yeah. I know ya need to do it and that's what bothers me. When ya need to do it, ya press and when ya press, ya screw up. And Jake, I wouldn't like it if ya screw up. I got too much to lose. And, so do ya."

He was right. I more than knew he was right. There was no way I wanted to endanger Ethan or Camille. If something went wrong… I was scared for what could happen to Ethan.

"Nothing is going to go wrong Mr. Villani. Do you remember when I first started with you? I was green. I knew nothing but you taught me and I learned quick. And, the profit was in the pudding."

Mr. Villani lifted his empty cup up and the waitress hustled over to fill it.

"You're right Jake. You were green. You were young and…you were naïve and carefree. Not no more buddy boy. Not no more."

He shook his head emphasizing his position.

"And besides, I got partners now and I got eyes watching me."

"Then let them watch us make money."

"It's not about the money, any more. I got plenty of money. Plenty of it. Back then it was about the money, not now. Now its about power and control."

"Power? Control of what?"

"Control of the group. Years ago seven of us

created this group. Now we operate as a collective. Each of us operates our business in our own right but operate collectively in opportunities that we wouldn't have individually. The power is important because it enables me to have control over what the collective gets involved in. The power comes from our scorecard of individual operations. It's not just about the money, other factors involved. And one of them is not screwing up. And Jake, these guys mean business."

My palms were sweating.

"So the question becomes, how can I help you gain more power within the group? And you know I can help you do that."

"Jake, you are one persistent bastard. And I like that but ---"

"No buts---"

He quickly held up his hand. I realized people could be watching. I showed respect.

He said, "Yeah, there are two buts. But one is, ya don't want your butt in the slammer. And but two is, ya don't want to butt heads with the group. Frankly, I don't know which would be worse."

My heart was racing, my hands were still sweating and my mouth was dry.

"But Mr. Villani...I know I can handle it and I'll start immediately doing exactly what you say. You guided me once. I know you can do it again."

"Once again, you are a persistent bastard."

"And light years ahead of that Nick guy you got working at the car lot. If you trust him, you can sure trust me."

The waitress came over and this time took my

empty plate.

She asked me, "Would you like some more coffee or anything else?"

"No thanks."

"Mr. Villani. Would you like anything else?"

Louie shook his head.

"You're one huge piece of work Jake Shaw. What the hell am I going to do with ya?"

"So then, we got a deal?"

"Let me think about it."

I moved a little closer to him, lowered my head and whispered.

"With all due respect Mr. Villani. No fucking way. Lets do it."

He sat back in his chair, laughed, and then put out his hand. This time to shake my hand.

"Ya win Jake, Ya win. Just don't fuck up. Ya hear me?

He stood up and we headed for the door. Everyone nodded their respect to him and wished him a wonderful day. We walked into the parking lot and I realized we didn't pay the check. He saw the puzzled look on my face.

He pointed his thumb back over his shoulder toward the Sunrise Café.

"I own the joint."

We had a deal but I wasn't sure what it was or if it was really a good thing. I wasn't sure at all. Not at all.

CHAPTER 15

Two days had passed since my frustrating walk with Odin. No one could accuse him of wasting words. It was a mystery to me, why I felt impelled to see him again. My reasoning mind told me to forget him but my intuition urged me on and I listened. I checked the clock it was 8:25. I needed to hustle to get to the park on time.

When I arrived at the park, he was walking off in the distance. There was no time to waste, so I ran to catch up with him.

"Good morning Odin. Sorry I'm late."

He gave a small smile.

"Can we continue our talk about the universe?" I asked.

He nodded in the affirmative.

"So where in space do we go today Odin?"

"Homework. Did you do it?"

My breath caught. "It's been so busy I didn't have time to do it. But I'm here today, ready to go."

He didn't respond. We walked without speaking for half the loop before I had enough silence.

"So Odin, are you going to continue?"

"No."

"And...why not?"

"No homework."

I was getting pissed. "Come on Odin, I understood what you said. I didn't need to study up on it."

He stopped walking, turned to face me, and stung me with his eyes. Then in a gravely voice said. "Understand, that to know but not yet to do is not really to know."

"What?"

"Remember, wasn't it was necessary to understand addition and subtraction before you got to multiplication and division?"

"Well I ---."

He grimaced and shook his head. "No homework tells me, you don't want this understanding enough."

I walked for a while without rebuttal.

"So now what?" I asked.

"Life is an inside game. You need to do your homework."

We walked the rest of the path in silence and when we reached the end, he just kept walking out of the park as he did the last time. And I, like I did the last time, began a sprint around the park. Again frustrated and wondering, what the hell?

***

"Ethan, how many cookies you want?"

"I'm hungry. Can I have six?"

"Six? You'll have more sugar in you than a sugar cane."

"Five?"

"You were going for five anyway, right?"

He laughed. "Can't blame a kid for trying."

I pulled out six Oreo cookies from the box. After all, it was Friday afternoon and I wanted to reward the kid for trying.

"And you're having milk with the cookies. No soda."

"Yes sir."

I opened the refrigerator and pulled out the milk. Like the rest of the refrigerator, it was just about empty but there was enough milk to fill the glass. I needed to go food shopping but hated to part with the money.

"Hey dad, a guy just got out of a black car and he's walking up the driveway."

I went to the living room, looked out the window and saw a black Mercedes convertible and a man approaching the house. He knocked on the door. I delayed. He knocked, harder. I opened it and before me stood a man about six feet tall, impeccably dressed in black linen pants to match his black linen shirt, which set off his silver hair and his silver goatee. He was elegant except for the arrogant look on his face.

"About time you answered the door," he said in a faded French accent.

My neck recoiled. "How can I help you?"

"I want to see the inside of your house."

"You do, do you?"

"My name is Leon Dijon. I am going to be the new

holder of your mortgage and I'm here to inspect your house."

"You're who? And you're what?"

"I have already told you once. My name is Dijon, Leon Dijon. I want to inspect your house."

"You need to call Frank Mangello and set up an appointment."

"No I don't. I'm here now and I want to see it".

He moved forward attempting to cross the threshold entering the house. I raised my hand and almost touched his chest. It backed him off. I noticed Ethan was watching. " Ethan, please go to your room."

"Yes sir."

I looked at this character and moved across the threshold to the outside. This forced him to back up. I closed the door behind me.

"Listen, whoever the hell you are. I don't care what you want, or what you think you're doing here, I suggest you back your ass up."

He was obviously not disturbed by my suggestion.

"You are Jake Shaw aren't you?"

He damn well knew who I was.

"I repeat. I am Leon Dijon. I am buying the mortgage to this house from Frank Mangello very soon. As it stands now, you are two payments behind in your mortgage. I assume shortly that number will be three. At the time of closing with Mangello I will become your mortgage holder and you'll be three payments in arrears. If I were you, I would let me inspect this house. And that means, now." He smirked. "So, we can get off on a good start. Do you understand Mr. Jake Shaw?"

My whole body tightened. "Let me get something clear. Did you just threaten me?"

"I will repeat this one last time. I am Leon Dijon and it's in your best interest to let me inspect this house immediately."

"First of all you arrogant bastard, this house, is my home. Second, and I repeat, I don't give a shit who you think you are, what you think you're going to do or what you want. But if you don't want those fine threads you're wearing to get ruined, it's in your best interests to get your ass off my property before I pick you up and physically throw your ass to the curb. And don't think for a second I can't or I won't do it."

Dijon backed up three steps. "Mr. Shaw enjoy your home while you can because in a short while I will be in control of what happens to this house. And I'm sure you won't be happy about that."

Dijon turned around and strutted to his car. I followed him at a distance to make sure the pompous ass kept going. He got in his car and quickly drove off.

I hustled into Ethan's room. He was standing by the window with a scared look on his face.

"Dad, who was that man? Are we going to lose our home? Do we have to leave? I don't want to move. I like it here."

I put my arms around him, picked him up and looked straight in his eyes.

"No son, we're not moving. We're staying right here. You and me, together. I promise you that."

"Good. I like it when you promise me something cause I know you'll keep your promise." He threw his arms around my neck. "I love you dad."

"Hey buddy, you never did get to eat those six cookies."

"Six? You gave me six? You're the best." He jumped off me and ran to the kitchen.

I stood and looked around his room, and thought of Dijon and my fists tightened. It was good thing I kept myself in check. Years ago I would have left Dijon in pieces lying in the street. Those were the good old days. Not a care in the world. Now, I've plenty to care about and I'm not going to let anything bad happen to who and what I care about. There was no way that was going to happen. And this time I wasn't going to let Villani Enterprises down either.

***

A glance at the clock reminded me it was 2 a.m. and I was sitting in bed wide-awake as my mind whirled with thoughts of my experience with Dijon, the possibilities with Louie and there was Odin. Odin was a mystery but once again my gut encouraged me to deal with him. So after getting up to go to the bathroom, I plopped down on the bed and began to contemplate the universe. I thought, what the hell.

CHAPTER 16

"Homework?"

"Yes Odin, I did my homework and believe it or not I enjoyed it."

He simply nodded his approval, walking straight ahead watching a pelican crash into the bay hoping to snag a fish for breakfast.

"So can we continue our discussion?" I asked.

Again, he nodded.

"Odin, I wasn't exactly sure how to begin so I reviewed what you said the other day and then went on the internet. You're right there's a ton of information to explore. I began to read but after a while, my mind floated into space, sort of meditating, and then it felt like I was surfing the universe. At one point, I visualized Earth as a blue and white ornament dangling on a Christmas tree. It was amazing.

The longer I surfed, the more I wanted to learn, the more I learned about the vastness of universe, the more fascinated I became and the more I enjoyed surfing the universe. It was a wonderful cycle. In some way it was weird, because I got a sense of the insignificance of my tiny place in the universe but at the same time, I also got a sense of my own inner power. I can't really describe it in words. You just have to do it for yourself. Now I sound like you. Funny eh?"

"Anything else?"

"Plenty," I laughed. "There's a boatload of information that would bore a science class but was exhilarating when I surfed it. Like the Sun being 93 million miles away from here and we can fit about a million Earths in it. And hell get this, as big as it is, the Sun is only an average star up there in the sky. There's a giant star up there called, VY Canis Major that can fit 2100 suns into it! That was way beyond my ability even to surf it."

"What else excited you?"

"I'm incredibly intrigued by the universe being almost 14 billion years old. That's a lot of candles on a birthday cake. And when I think of the Earth being around for 4.5 billion years, well that's just a huge amount of years we're talking about. When I reflect on me getting older, it becomes funny, it's so inconsequential in the large scheme of things.

I have to admit it, surfing the universe is much different than just thinking about facts and information. It's like having your own little experience, your own adventure. I'll tell you, the next time I see a sunset, I'm going to know that the little orange fireball ball on the horizon is 4.5 billion years old and is 93 million miles away. The reality of that visual is a little mind boggling."

"Is there more that moved you?"

"Here's the big one. I'm absolutely fascinated with how the universe got started. Where did the entire place come from?"

"Well, the widely held scientific theory of how the universe began is called the Big Bang which postulates the universe began from a single atom called the singularity."

"Yes, I read about that. But science has no idea of where this singularity, this singular atom came from or what ignited it. That's what really, really intrigues me."

Odin laughed gently and said, "That's the greatest of all mysteries isn't it?"

I continued. "I also read about the cosmological First Cause argument that everything has to have a cause but science has no idea of the first cause of the singularity."

"Perhaps it's because the first cause is beyond the parameters of science, beyond a physical dimension. As human beings we are sensate creatures. We input information mostly through our senses. If we can't see it, hear it, touch it, taste it or smell it, as far as we're concerned it doesn't exist. And if science can't do the same, including count it and measure it, then whatever it might be, it simply isn't. But there is a reality beyond which we can normally sense."

"How so?"

"For instance, dogs can hear things way beyond our human capacity to hear. They can also smell things that, perhaps thankfully, we can't smell. And eagles can see acutely for long distances."

"True."

"So perhaps consider a first cause is beyond our human capacity to understand."

"So are you talking about God?"

"Jake, understand there is something, an ineffable power that sourced the singularity and ignited it. Science may not know what it is, but science has come to understand that everything is energy and this energy permeates, animates and fills our universe with a vast intelligence and creative energy."

"Are you calling this energy God?"

"I simply call it Source. And at times I call it Spirit because its essence is invisible. I prefer not to call it God because the term has many connotations and beliefs associated with it, which can get confusing."

"I understand."

Two dolphins cut through the surface of the bay and jumped in the air. Perhaps they wanted to hear more too.

"Jake, it's easy to observe that the universe operates in perfect order. On a daily basis we know exactly what time the sun will rise and set in each part of the earth. Every year the four seasons happen at the same time. Every year flowers bloom at the same time and crops get harvested at the same time. And we expect it to happen because empirically, we know it as happened each year.

On a larger scale, look at our solar system. It also appears in perfect order. Every year the planets continue their orbit in an expected progression. Not only that, but science can also determine the exact placement of the planets far into the future. Such perfect order demands that there is an incredible intelligence at work, an intelligence that sourced and maintains the universe.

This incomprehensible intelligent creative energy is the key to the millions of forms of diverse life including the water, the land, the trees, plants, animals and the billions of humans on the planet, including you Jake. Mystics knew this, eons ago and science has been growing to understand that the mystics were far ahead of the rest of us. It's indeed a mystical mystery.

The sad thing is most people pay little to no attention to this Source intelligence. Most people give more awareness to a football game or a movie than they give to the essence of their own life. If they get lucky, something clicks in their consciousness and they become more aware, or they get jolted by a bump in the road of life, they can get a wake up call."

"So we're back to a wake up call."

We were coming to the end of the loop but I wanted to hear more. I was surprised to hear Odin talk as much. Perhaps he felt my enthusiasm to learn more; that could be part of it but I also sensed this was something he lived deeply, felt strongly about and wanted to share. Nevertheless, I was expecting another homework assignment. He looked at his watch.

"Jake do you have another couple of minutes?"

"I sure do."

"I want to emphasize this point. People are so focused on the matters of the world, that they're ignorant of, or simply not mindful of the brilliance of Source energy actually animating their being. For whatever reason they fail to cultivate their Source essence and the true power of their own lives. It's like driving a car never thinking about filling it with gas. That's not smart.

Spirit dwells in every thing on this beautiful earth, in our glorious solar system, in the vastness of the universe. We can't truly understand it but we can sense its presence. We can sense its presence by observing life. See that beautiful parrot on the branch or the tree itself, both have the same non-physical, Source essence of life within it. That man and woman sitting on the bench or those dolphins that jumped out of the water or that dog running over there, all gifted with the same Source essence of life, that 13.7 billion years ago sparked that singularity.

Hear it in the birds singing. Taste it in your food, Smell it in the flowers or feel it when you hug a loved one. Jake you can draw near to it by contemplating its existence in life around you. And as you look deeper into the life around you, it will reveal its splendor to you."

"Odin, I think I know my next homework assignment. Observe Source, the spiritual essence of life in all that I see, hear, touch, smell and taste and especially within every person I see, including myself. Right?"

He didn't answer my question. He just walked away in silence but...but for the first time, I saw a full smile on his face.

I still didn't have a clue where this was going or how it was going to help me with my situation but I did know one thing, I felt at peace. And it felt damn good.

CHAPTER 17

"Man, it's a perfect Saturday afternoon for baseball. Seventy-two degrees, not a cloud in the sky and the grass looks as smooth as my ex-wife's ass," Blackie said.

I laughed. "I wouldn't know about your ex-wife's ass but it is a great day for baseball. And that, I do know."

"Ya better not know about my ex-wife's ass," Blackie laughed. "But, speaking of asses, what's the bug up yours?"

"What do you mean?"

"Jake, Jake don't give me that shit. You've had some bug biting yours the whole time you've been here."

"You're one subtle dude, aren't you?"

"Subtlety was never my strong suit on the job. Now give."

I brushed him off. "It's a long story."

"Then cut it short. Hey, you know when I smell blood I'm in for the kill. Give."

I hesitated for a moment. "I've got a private mortgage on my house. It's with a guy named Frank Mangello."

"Yeah, I met him at a party at your house. Nice guy."

"He's having financial difficulties and he needs to sell my mortgage."

"So that's not such a big deal. What else?"

"You're a smart cop, Dick Tracy."

"You're a smart ass, Jake Shaw and you're trying to avoid the issue and it ain't going to happen. Continue. What else?"

"One of the guys who wants to buy mortgage paid me a visit yesterday."

"From your tone, I can smell him already. Smells like dog shit. "

"You got it."

"How big a pile?"

"Not sure yet but big. He's one pompous, arrogant piece of work."

"I met plenty of his type."

"He showed up at the door and demanded that I let him inspect the house. Immediately! When I told him to hit the streets, he tried to intimate me with threats that after he bought the mortgage my life would be miserable."

"Oh brother, you're a guy I wouldn't suggest threatening."

"Like you said, if the batter was crowding the plate, I wouldn't be shy about throwing a high and tight fastball to move him back off the plate."

"Now, let me push just a little more?"

"Is this your sweet side detective?"

"Yes sir. Ain't it gentle?"

"Go ahead push some more."

"Besides being an arrogant asshole, what else about this guy bugs you? What's this jerks name? "

"His name is Leon Dijon. All I know about him is that he's a Frenchman who's been in Sarasota for awhile. Mangello thinks he's bad news. Besides that I'm not sure. Something else bugs me. I get this uncomfortable feeling. Like there's more to this then a mortgage deal."

"Like what?"

"Like, he drives a black 550 Mercedes convertible."

"Sweet, but not particularly disturbing other than the asshole can afford it."

"Here's the rub. Last week when I was pulling away from Ethan's school after I dropped him off, I hesitated for a few seconds and bent to pickup a book off the passenger's side floor and when I got back up and began to go, this black 550 Mercedes convertible came out of nowhere, almost side swiped me, then bolted down the street. I now believe it was Dijon."

Blackie sat straight up on the bleachers, like an animal on alert.

I continued. "It makes no sense. What purpose would it serve him if he hit me?"

"Jake, the reality is that sense doesn't rule the day. People do a lot of off the wall things. I know. I made a living from it. Some appear perfectly normal, but they're far from normal. They can be way out to lunch."

"Ain't that the truth. Look Ethan's coming up to

bat."

Ethan strolled into the batter's box, adjusted his helmet and took a few warm up swings.

"Damn Jake, he looks like a pro."

My heart swelled. I smiled proud. Ethan swung at the first pitch and drilled a line drive down the left field line. It was foul.

"We worked on his batting during the winter at the batting cages. He even started to switch hit."

A glum look smeared Blackie's face.

"You miss Bobby, don't you?" I asked.

"Big time," came Blackie's sullen response. "Doubly so during baseball season. I don't know if I can take another season like last year." He takes his Yankee baseball cap off and scratches his head. "More and more I've been looking on the internet for apartments in Brooklyn."

"I understand. I'd go nuts without Ethan. The kid's my life. How serious are you about going back?"

"More and more serious. I can go at any time. The guy who owns my condo is a good guy and he lets me stay there month to month, even if it's against the association rules. He feels good having an ex-cop there. So I'm good to stay. And, I got an old buddy in Brooklyn, who'll let me stay with him until I get my own place; so I'm good to go."

Ethan hit another foul ball, this time down the right field line.

"The kid's a spray hitter, the dangerous type, able to go with the pitch. Solid hitter," Blackie commented like a baseball announcer.

"What would you do with your furniture?"

"Hell, I'd give most of it to Goodwill. Not much I want to keep. For what I want to keep, I'd rent a little trailer, hook it up to the back of my truck. Then one night before dawn, I'd be gone."

Ethan pounded a solid grounder foul of third base.

"What about your friends down here?"

"Jake, I've been slow to make friend down here. I don't play golf. Damn sure don't play tennis and I'm no old man in the sea; sitting on a boat fishing drives me nuts. My play was always my work. For Christ's sake you're my only real friend down here. The guys at Moe's are just time spenders."

"Good thing you like baseball," I interjected.

"Yeah, I do love my baseball." Blackie agreed. When I…if I go, you and Ethan can come to visit me, the four of us can go to Yankee Stadium and root for the Yankees."

"Just as long as they're not playing the Rays. Ethan and I both are Tampa Bay Rays fans to the max. Go Rays."

Ethan hit a deep fly ball that kept rising until it sailed over the cyclone fence in left field.

"Damn the kid hit a home run!" Blackie screamed. "A damn home run."

I stood quietly, clapping a proud father's clap and watched him round the bases. I sucked in the glorious moment until I saw it. Beyond the fence was a black 550 Mercedes convertible. I grabbed Blackie by the arm and pointed out beyond the fence.

"See that Mercedes? That's Dijon."

A scowl crossed Blackie's face, "What the hell is he doing here? Buddy boy, I don't like this shit. Not at all.

This ain't good. Now, I'm really getting heated."

And my stomach felt like there was a chunk of ice in it and the water was dripping through my veins.

***

It was 7:53 p.m. I was a few minutes early. I sat in my car, and thought of Ethan's home run... my kid hitting a homer. He was ecstatic. I was ecstatic. Then, I remembered Dijon behind the fence and Blackie's remark. Son of a bitch. I opened the car door and headed up to Camille's condo. I was not in any mood to go to party. Not even in the mood to see Camille. What I felt like doing was finding Dijon and...

Before I could knock, she opened the front door. She looked stunning, absolutely gorgeous. I took her in my arms and held her tight.

"I've missed you," she whispered in my ear.

Confusion rushed through me like a flash flood. I didn't know what I was feeling. But I did know that I didn't want to let her go. Then she said, "We better get going cowboy, we don't want to miss anything."

She looked at me, but mis-read my sullen face. "Don't worry baby, we'll get to what you want when we get home later. I promise. I said I missed you and that meant in more ways than one."

I smiled at that comment.

***

Fifteen minutes later we arrived at the party. Very quickly I realized this was going to be a long evening.

Camille quickly picked up on my attitude.

"Just bear with this for awhile, it'll be fun. Remember this could be important to me. There are lots of art buyers here tonight."

"I got it under control babe." I lied. Usually I did my mix, mingle and jingle dance but that night it wasn't happening.

An hour later, which felt like a week, Camille reconnected with me. She said. "This is one good crowd. How you doing? Better?"

"Worse. I'm ready to leave this hot dog stand."

"Come on Jake, where's your normal party attitude?"

"Maybe I need another drink."

Three drinks later, my struggle amplified into a war. I was getting angry; it was time to leave. I corralled Camille.

"I need to go. I'm done with being here."

"Just fifteen more minutes."

"Camille, I can't last another five minutes."

I saw her disappointment and annoyance. But I had to leave.

"Okay—okay. Give me a minute to say some quick good byes and we'll leave."

My alcohol content was high, so Camille drove home, The ride was as silent as funeral precession. When we got in Camille's condominium, her emotion found its voice.

"Last week I know I said, I'd give you room to work through whatever it is you're working through but I need you to work with me Jake. I love you but sometimes lately, you're making it hard to like you and that's starting to scare me. You say you love me. You knew this party was important to me but you were obviously not the least bit cooperative tonight."

"Listen I ---."

"Right now Jake, I don't want to hear what you have to say. I need you to listen. I barely speak to you all week. I miss you terribly and tonight you act like the last place in the world you want to be is with me. I simply don't get it."

My thinking was fuzzy with stress and alcohol. I was dead ass tired and I was stone silent.

"You haven't been yourself in months. And tonight was horrible. Horrible. I needed to talk to people and all I did was worry about you."

I've had enough and didn't want to listen anymore. I walked to the door to leave.

"Where are you going?"

"Home."

"Home? You can't drive. And why are you going home? Are you tired of me Jake? Tell me the truth Jake, are you tired of me?"

"I'm going home to be alone, just like you did last week."

"That's it. You're tired of me."

"No. I'm tired of me."

When I left, the wind slammed the door shut. I didn't mean to do that. Or did I? Right then, I really didn't care.

CHAPTER 18

After four hours of being with RH in his garage in Tampa, I understood how he got his name. RH stood for Reverse Houdini, because the guy could break into anything that had wheels and be on the road in less than a minute. Working with RH brought back memories. And the reality was the work was anything but boring. Still I just couldn't believe I was back at this after all these years. Back where I started, but not on the streets of Brooklyn. This time it would be on the streets of Sarasota.

The garage phone rang. RH answered it, "Yeah boss?" He turned and gave me the phone. "He wants to talk to you."

"Hello… No problem."

"Gotta go?" RH asked.

I nodded. "He wants to see me in his office before I head back to Sarasota. But I got a little time."

"Good, cause I got one more thing to show you. It's a beauty. Then I think you're ready to bust and roll."

***

Thirty minutes later I walked into the lobby of Louie's building. The pretty, smiling face of Ms. Roma greeted me. "Good afternoon Mr. Shaw. Go right up. Mr. Villani is waiting for you. Mr. Villani's secretary is out running some errands, so go directly into his office."

I knocked on the ten foot mahogany door, waited a moment and walked in. Louie was on the couch and older man was sitting in the arm chair.

"Jake, finally," Louie said.

"Sorry I'm a bit late. I was learning a cool technique from RH and wanted to get it right."

"Education is certainly important," Louie agreed. He stood up and swung his arm toward the older man. "Jake, Let me introduce ya to Mr. Joseph Bellino. Affectionately and respectfully known as Joe Bell. Joe Bell is an important man from New York. I wanted ya to meet each other while he's visiting Tampa."

I offered my hand to shake Joe Bell's hand. He gave me his left hand. His right hand hung limp at his side. He saw that I noticed and he simply said, "A bullet."

"Sit Jake, I have something to share with ya," Louie said.

"I'm all ears, Mr. Villani."

"Again, I want to say how fortunate we are to have Joe Bell here for this conversation. The entire organization values his wisdom and experience."

Joe Bell lips broke a small smile.

"I've been thinking a lot since our last meeting.

You're a good salesman Jake. I gotta give ya that. And I know I agreed to doing a deal with ya but," he scratched his head. "But to blunt, it wasn't without skepticism. So after ya left, I had to re-consider my position."

My stomach tightened. Was this slipping away too?

"Mr. Villani, let me say --"

Louie put up his hand and I held my tongue.

"Jake, listen."

I felt the hope drain out of me. But…but maybe this was for the best. At least there wouldn't be a chance, Ethan have to grow up with his father in the slammer.

"When ya first came to me, I was feeling old wounds. Ya hurt me and I don't like to be hurt. But I thought back to the beginning when ya started with me. Momma and I took ya in with an open heart. We treated ya like family. Ya were always a mix between a son and a little brother to me. But, ya fucked it up when ya left."

I grasped for a rope dangling from the sinking ship. "But---."

"No need to say anything. Is there Joe Bell?"

Joe Bell shook his head in agreement.

"Then when ya came the second time and ya start talking, I started to listen, not with a hurt heart but with a clear head. Funny thing, my heart started to heal. Go figure. So I kept thinking and thinking and this is what it comes around to. Here's the deal"

Louie stood up and walked over to his desk and picked up his cup of coffee. "Would either of ya like a cup?"

I wrestled with my impatience. What the hell was

coming?

"Jake, here's what I'm thinking. Three things. First, this business is growing fast. We're into a lot of things and we want to get into a lot more. Some of them are legit, some skirt the line and others, well others, ya know what I mean." He took a swig of coffee. " Second, about ya, funny thing I asked myself, 'what would Jesus do?' So now I'm looking at ya like a prodigal son or prodigal brother come home." Another swig of java. "And third, and this is strictly confidential. Only Joe Bell here knows, I'm having some health challenges. Nothing major we hope, but still I'm not what I used to be. But I'm still strong. But I can use some help, sort of a right hand man. Ain't that right Joe Bell?"

Joe Bell nodded in the affirmative.

"Okay 1, 2, 3. When I added them up, it added up to a lot. Right Joe Bell?"

This time Joe Bell squinted at me.

"It added up to this. Here's my deal. Ya come in and first ya do some procuring and get your feet wet. Then as fast as we're comfortable, I begin to teach ya how to run this organization. Step by step through all the ropes. You'll be able to make more money than you've ever imagined. Before that happens of course, ya and the kid need to move to Tampa. Sarasota is too far away. When you're needed you're needed right then, not an hour from then." He held up his hand. "Wait a second." He walked over to his desk and pulled out three fine Cuban cigars. He handed one to each of us. "Before, we light these babies to celebrate…Jake, I gotta tell ya this. I thought long and hard on this. I even talked to momma. I never thought a dead man could live again but there's still a place in my heart for ya, just don't fucking break it again. I'm warning ya. I won't be able to handle it this time."

Joe Bell stood up and looked me dead in my eyes. My body shivered. "I don't want his heart broken. Is that understood?"

"Understood."

Louie lit the cigars, "Let's celebrate with a smoke."

I couldn't believe what I just heard. I didn't know if I should celebrate or if I heard a death knell. What the hell just happened?

***

Driving back to Sarasota, my mind was going faster than the 90 mph on the speedometer. I was trying hard to get a handle on the situation with Louie. Sure it took the money pressure off me for the moment, but it held the possibility of burning in hell forever. Then I spotted a police car peeking out of the bushes. My heart rate quickened, my foot pushed down on the brake. I backed down to the speed limit. I glided up toward the police car. I was sure I was nailed. Sure he got me. But when I drove slowly by the parked black and white, it was empty. Empty. It was a decoy. A sigh bellowed from my belly. Safe. I breathed deeper. Then my phone rang. It was Mangello.

"Hi Frank. What's the news?"

"Strange news Jake, strange news."

"Like what?"

"Two days ago I had three qualified prospects,

seriously interested in buying your mortgage. Today, two out of the three act like they never spoke to me. I don't get it. Something is screwy. But I still have one and he's gun-ho and he wants to inspect your property as soon as possible."

My foot pushed down on the accelerator.

"It wouldn't be the French guy?"

"Yeah, it's him. How did you know?"

"The obnoxious bastard tried to plow his way into my house on Thursday and I was on the verge of physically kicking him to the curb. I don't like that son of a bitch."

"Jake…I need the money badly Jake. I need him to be able to inspect the house. Can he do it tomorrow?"

I needed time to get a handle on this situation. "No not tomorrow Frank. I can't do it tomorrow. Wednesday, Wednesday works. In the morning, say ten. I don't want Ethan to be there when he gets there. Wednesday at ten."

"Thanks Jake. I'll tell him. If there's any change I'll let you know."

What the hell else can go wrong? I glanced at the speed I was back at 90 mph again, so I brought it down to the speed limit and moved to the right lane. After I drove for a few miles, I relaxed a bit and forgot about the jerk Dijon. Louie's deal was beginning to look real good.

CHAPTER 19

Ethan had to be at school early, so I arrived at Bay Front Park at 8:15. I took a slow jog around the park. There wasn't another person in sight, I was alone. But not really. Ethan was with me, Camille too and Louie, as well as the rodent Dijon; they all had their places in my head. And, Odin would be there soon. The first loop around the park went easily, so I picked up the pace on the second loop. It felt good to go faster and burn off some tension. Soon people started to arrive. Mostly dog walkers with their doggie cleaning bags. Considerate of them. I approached the end of the loop and saw Odin looking at me.

I laughed and said, "Before you even ask me, yes I did my homework."

"Tell me about it."

Before I could begin, a loose dog ran in between us with its owner huffing and puffing after it. I took the time to gather myself.

"Well to be upfront, it wasn't easy. When I practiced

being aware of Source energy in the trees, plants, flowers and even the people, it was much easier than when I tried to conceptualize it within myself. I could observe and get a handle on an energy that animated others, sort of like everything was operating off a battery but I couldn't find the battery within me."

Odin stopped walking and pointed to a bench along the water. "Let's sit over there."

"Do you feel okay?" I asked concerned.

"Yes, I feel fine. Why do you ask?"

"Because, we never sat before. We always walked at a good clip."

We got to the bench and sat down. Before us the bay was calm and in the distance was a view of the beautiful Ringling Bridge.

"Jake I want to sit, so we can more easily focus on what we're going to talk about because it's the most important thing you can do in your life. And it will foster the biggest transformation you will ever make. And yes of course, it will be process, a process, which will take desire, dedication and discipline. However, the rewards will be more than worth the effort. And personally, my biggest regret is that I didn't get started sooner in my life."

"I'm all ears. All ears."

He took a deep breath and smiled. It was if a deep peace washed over him and cleansed his regret.

"Jake, there is indeed a Source of all that flows through the entire universe. Science can't exactly prove what it is yet, but our soul knows it. That is, if we listen to it. It speaks to us not in words but in a sense of knowing and feeling. And no, we can't see it because it is Spirit, but we can see it express through all that we do see, in the millions of forms on this planet. Without it nothing would exist. Life does have an essence and Source energy is that essence.

What I want to deeply express to you today is that Spirit is not just within you Jake, but it is you Jake, expressing as you. All that you are is because of its expression through you. You breathe its breath, you see through its eyes, you love through its heart. Spirit within you, as you, is the same Source that sparked the big bang. And with this divine spark comes all the peace, power, love, beauty, joy, wisdom and abundance that you can say yes to. Source power animates your life. Call it your Higher Power, if you choose. Without your Higher Power, you Jake, don't exist. When you die, we say you 'expired.' This is because Spirit, your Higher Power has exited your body. Source, Spirit, Higher Power are all different terms we use to try express the Ineffable."

"Isn't God one of those terms too?"

"Yes of course it is. Jake, call it whatever you want, but make sure you call it. Make it personal to you, develop and cultivate a relationship with it. Be mindful of its presence within you. It will serve you because in serving you, it serves itself as it expresses through you. That's the reason you exist Jake. You're here as an expression of your Higher Power on this planet. That's why we're all here. When I began to understand that truth, my life changed in wonderful ways I couldn't have imagined. And it's still happening. Like I said, I wish I had started sooner."

His face could have been the poster for world

peace. I had never seen anything like it. I wanted it.

"Odin, tell me what to do?"

"Understand Jake, there is no one way to embody this experience because you are different from me, we all are different, so there isn't exactly one way to embrace Spirit within you but I will make a strong suggestion."

My stomach turned as I thought to ask this question.

"Odin, before you make the suggestion, and I really hate to ask this question. It seems so trivial and meaningless in this conversation. But…will this help me in my situation?"

His laughter surprised me. "Be patient Jake and you will in due time, see how vital this conversation is but first stay with me. Be here now. Deal?"

"Deal."

" Now as I continue, I will be redundant only because this is such an important realization to embrace. And, I'm going to try to make it as simply as I can."

"I'm ready. Let'r rip."

"Whether you are aware of it or not, you already have a relationship with whatever you choose to call it, Source, Spirit, God or your Higher Power. It is the most intimate relationship you have because without it Jake, you don't exist. The relationship you have with Spirit is the essence of your life. Most people are not aware of this relationship, they are focused on the day to day matters of life, however they may see them. Again I say, most people need a wake up call to jolt them out of this sensate world. If they get a wake up call, however, that doesn't mean they answer it. They don't have to say, 'Hello,' to a relationship with Spirit, they can just continue to continue and get through whatever the crisis they're hoping to get out of it. So far Jake, you've chosen to say hello."

"Hello, hello. What's next?"

"Like any other relationship you have in your life, whether, it's your wife, your partner, your child, your parent you need to cultivate it. Your Higher Power is already fully present in this relationship. Again, it's the essence of your life and it's waiting for you to wake up, join in and do your part to cultivate the relationship. Make it personal to you and see what happens. Although it's not a physical form, it is spiritually with you, as you. Be with it, talk with it as you would a person, after all it's the most important relationship you'll ever have and… it's forever."

"Do it like when I was a kid, having an imaginary friend? That's strange."

"It's only strange because you are so attached to the physical world. You're not yet used to the spiritual side of life. Once you start to cultivate this relationship, you will begin to feel it beyond your senses."

"Okay. Okay. How do I begin to cultivate this imaginary or spiritual relationship?"

"Since you're in a physical human form, it might be easier to relate to it as a person in physical form. You could try to embrace your Higher Power as a loving parent. You can choose it as your father, your mother or at different times switch genders. At all times this parent is loving, benevolent, powerful, generous and with any other qualities you choose."

"What if my actual parents weren't around or what if they weren't so wonderful?"

"Then give your Higher Power parent the qualities that you needed and wanted in your parent. And, Jake have no doubt those qualities are truly present in your Higher Parent."

"Qualities like?"

"Choose them as you would prefer them. Perhaps you would like to trust your parent for your good or be able to go to your parent for guidance. With whatever qualities you desire, your Higher Parent will be perfect for you and you can trust it."

"That's hard to accept. The only person I ever trusted was Molly and she left me."

"I'm sure her passing was tremendously hard to accept. She did however, play an important role in your waking up and raising your consciousness. Your new awareness of your relationship with your Higher Power will take time to develop. But I promise you, if you develop it, you'll be so glad you did. Jake, understand that Source energy was with you before you were you, and will be with you after Jake is no longer Jake. You have nothing to lose and everything to gain."

"It's just weird. How do I know it exists?"

"Do what you've already started doing and observe Spirit's essence of life in every creature you see. That big black dog by the tree, the woman who's walking the dog, the tree they're near, the red flower the dog is smelling, all have the essence of life within them. They just don't realize it. The dog, the tree and flower for sure are not aware of it. Perhaps the woman has such awareness. As for you Jake, you have the same Source energy within you giving you life. You can be sure of that because if you didn't you wouldn't be alive. Having that awareness, it's now up to you choose whether you want to cultivate your relationship. Then, do you have the determination to follow through and develop it?"

"Okay I choose to cultivate it. Now what do I do?"

"Love it."

"What? Love it? How can I love something I don't know and can't even see? How do I do that?"

"Yes love the ineffable. Imagine it as you choose, as a loving parent as I suggest or as the spark, the bright light within you. It is certainly both. Love it, as you want to be loved. Love it with the same passion as you love your son, because that's how your Higher Power loves you and more. Your love is finite. Your Higher Power's love is infinite and unconditional."

"My love for Ethan is beyond words."

"How would you like to be loved beyond words?"

"That's so unimaginable, it takes my breath away."

"And I see it welled your eyes."

I sighed. "Yes it did."

"Jake be mindful of Spirit's essence in your life and practice feeling that unimaginable love you just felt. You and your Higher Power are really one in the same. You are Onederful."

"Wonderful?"

"I don't mean wonderful in the normal sense, and of course, yes, that you are as well. But what I mean is O-n-e-d-e-r-f-u-l. Onederful, as in you both are one. You and Spirit are Onederful."

"Being Onederful."

"Yes Jake, be mindful of your union. Practice being aware of it. Contemplate it daily. Meditate it on it before you go to sleep and upon awakening. Be observant of Source's energy in all creatures you see and hear. Science tells us there's energy in even inanimate objects like that stone. Now for sure that stone doesn't have the mindfulness to cultivate its energy but you do and you can be open to the relationship you have with it. That's what the wake up call is all about."

"But Odin---"

"Before you ask your question, I will tell you how it affects your situation next time. But for now your homework is most important thing to do."

"Cultivate, develop your relationship with your Higher Power. And before I forget, let me tell you that I found it extremely helpful to give my Higher Power, the Spirit within me a name. I suggest you try it."

"A name? What's your Higher Power's name?"

"That's between me and my Higher Power. It's our sacred secret."

"Gotcha."

"Jake you've got to diligently do your homework because no homework means---"

"I know Odin. I know. No homework means no progress. What's my homework?"

"Practice being Onederful."

"Being Onederful. I like that. I can do that."

CHAPTER 20

At 11:a.m. I pulled into the parking lot of Munroe Realty. Robert Munroe's car was parked in its usual spot. I had to make some hard decisions and I needed bottom line, straight talk information and Robert Munroe was the guy to do it.

The receptionist greeted me with a smile as I approached her desk.

"Hi Mr. Shaw. It's good to see you."

"Maggie, when are you going to stop calling me Mr. Shaw and just call me Jake?"

"I don't know Mr. Shaw, she giggled. "I guess, I'll have to work on it."

"I'm counting on it. Is Robert in his office? I need to talk with him."

"Mr. Munroe is on a conference call. He told me not to disturb him."

"Any idea how long it might be?"

"Sorry. Not a clue."

"I'll wait a bit. Any coffee in the break room?"

"I just made a fresh pot. Help yourself, Mr…… I mean Jake."

"Thanks Maggie. Please let me know when he gets off the phone."

"Of course, of course."

The break room hadn't changed a bit since the last time I was in it, which was about two years. Then the market was hot and business was strong and I didn't have time to take a break and when it cooled down, I didn't need a break, I needed business.

The smell of the coffee drew my attention. I poured a cup and pulled up a chair. Through the window the Sun State Bank sign loomed large, reminding me I really needed money, a whole lot of it.

A big photograph of Munroe Realty associates with Robert front and center hung on the wall. Over the years Robert had built himself a solid reputation and a prosperous business. I wondered how he was doing in this tight market. Knowing Robert, he'd probably stashed a bundle of dough away. That's what I was doing until the economy started to eat up my small stash.

Ten minutes later, the door to the break room opened. I was surprised to see Robert Munroe.

"Hey Jake, did I startle you?"

"Yes, kind of. I wasn't expecting you so soon."

"The call wrapped up quicker than I thought it would. So here I am. How can I help you?"

"Robert, I need to ask you a couple of questions."

"Let's go into my office."

I followed him into his office, shut the door behind us and sat in a chair in front of his desk. He nodded and pointed to the couch.

"Let's sit on the couch. When you're ready, ask away."

I took a swig of coffee.

"As we both know I need to generate more income, so I was thinking of sitting more open houses. And before I forget, thank you for recommending me to Paul Langrock about his open house."

"I called it as I saw it. To bad it didn't work out for the both of you."

"Me too, but with open houses in mind... right now I don't have any of my own listings, if possible I would like to arrange holding open houses for the listings of other associates. Would that be feasible and could you arrange it?"

"The answer to both questions is, of course. What price range are you thinking?"

"I'm not sure, I'd like to check and see what is moving the best, if anything."

"Jake to be honest, I don't know myself. Sales have been all over the board. I'd say pick the properties you like best and give it a whirl."

"Fair enough."

"What else?"

"This one is a bottom line question."

"Shoot. I'm ready."

"Robert, you've been in this business a long time. You've lived through the market cycles. I don't want your pep rally assessment of the market. I need your gut, forecast. How long is this market going to be down?"

He got up from the couch and walked over to his

desk, picked up a yellow pad with notes on it and walked back to me.

"Jake, the conference call I was just on was with a group of my old cronies in the real estate business. A few local guys, some guys across the state and others spread across the country. The call ended a lot quicker than I thought because there was a clear consensus of opinion. In all our combined years and experiences, no one has seen the likes of the debacle we're in. The real estate industry is the lowest since the depression of almost one hundred years ago. It's a financial fiasco and worse it's been a human disgrace. There's guilt to be spread across the board from the government, to bankers, to mortgage brokers to builders, to buyers and owners. So to answer your question from my gut bottom line truth, I simply have no idea. And I'm like you, and so many others who played by the rules, totally angry about it. I wish I could give you a clear and more positive answer but Jake, all I know... all we know for sure is, it will take awhile."

Without even looking at his pad he threw it back to his desk. I'd never seen him even close to this frustrated.

He continued. "And to be real frank about the open house situation, in normal times it can be incredibly successful. In these times unless you have a cash buyer, ready to deal, the chances of you finding financing for a buyer is exceedingly slim."

I assumed that. He just confirmed it. But at least I knew for sure what I was dealing with.

"Just so I'm perfectly clear, you see no clear time frame for this mess to clean itself up?"

"No Jake, I don't. Wish I could but I can't."

"Thank you for being so honest with me. I expected nothing else even though I was hoping for your outlook to be something different. I'll give more thought to the open house situation and be back to you. And Robert..."

"Yes?"

"You're a noble man. It's my pleasure to work with you."

I left the office, walked to my car and settled in the seat. I kept thinking about going back to work for Louie. My mind told me it was the only rope left to hang on to, but my gut said differently. Yet, I saw no other options, no other way.

My phone rang. It was Camille.

"Hey beautiful, how are you?"

"Jake, I'm not good."

"What's going on?'

"I want to talk... need to talk... tomorrow when I get there. I want to reserve that time for talk. I need to. Do you understand?"

"Okay love, I hear you. Count me in. We can talk."

"Good. Good bye. See you tomorrow."

It was short but not sweet. And Camille was always sweet, well most always. Then I remembered I had that jerk Dijon coming tomorrow too. It was going to be one hell of a day.

CHAPTER 21

It was ten minutes before Dijon was due. I hated the thought of him in my home, walking through the rooms and inspecting whatever he'll be inspecting. It made my blood boil. It violated my being to have a creep like that in my home, in something I've invested in and labored long and hard to renovate. There wasn't a nook or cranny in the house that I didn't know about it. If Frank Mangello wasn't such a stand up guy, who treated Ethan and I with an open heart, Dijon wouldn't get his ass close to this place.

When I was renovating the house, the city inspector assigned to the job was a hard ass. The guy acted like I was the enemy. Talk about having a hornets nest up your butt, he must have had two up his. One day I told Frank how much trouble I was having with this guy. Frank asked me his name and I told him. The next time the guy inspected the house, he was like a different human being. He was cordial, even friendly. I wondered what was up. One day he said to me,

"Frank Mangello told me you are a good guy and that you do what you say you're going to do. Nice to meet you."

From that day forward his whole approach to the job was different. Before the renovation was over, we were having beers together. Mangello never said a word to me about it. From then on, if Frank Mangello needed my help, he had it. Even if Dijon was a rodent.

Two minutes later, I heard the rodent knock on the front door. I opened the door and saw Dijon dressed like he spent way too much time getting ready. Once again, a mono-chrome man. Silver shoes, pants, belt and shirt, the same silver manicured goatee. Along side of him, stood a tall, skinny dweeb with a tape measure, a pad and a clipboard.

"This is Peter Gorman," Dijon said.

With that terse introduction, they entered the house and took a few steps into the living room.

"No need to show us around the house. We prefer privacy," Dijon declared.

It felt like hot lava slithered through my body. "First of all friend, this is my home and not a house. And second, I'll decide how much privacy, you're offered."

"First of all Mr. Shaw, I'm not your friend and not inclined to be your friend. But there's no need to get aggressive. And second, think of this as a small price to pay for the slight possibility of you keeping your precious home and it is only a slight possibility. It's not my fault you're not capable of handling your responsibilities. Now is it?"

I stepped toward the asshole with a clenched first but a knock at the door diverted my attention. I wasn't expecting anyone. I reversed my path and opened the door.

"Hey Jake, my boy. How are you doing?" Blackie stood in the doorway, like a soldier on guard duty staring directly at Dijon. "Excuse me, I didn't realize you had company."

"What are you doing here?" I asked.

"Man, I had way too much coffee at my breakfast meeting and I was on my way home but I knew I'd never make it, so I decided to stop here and take a leak. I'll only be a minute. Excuse me."

I turned back to the rodent and his dweeb. They gazed around for a few minutes whispering, but I still heard Dijon say, "It's nice but small. No need to continue here."

Gorman mumbled back. "Too small for what you want to do."

My fist clenched again, my jaw tightened and I took a deep breath just as Blackie re-entered the room.

"That's better. A whole lot better," Blackie shared.

"May we go into the bedrooms?" Dijon sneered.

I led the way into my room.

Gorman said, "Sizeable with a lot of windows."

I watched Dijon act as if he was a detective looking for clues, trying to size the area up. He stared with anger in his eyes at the bed for a moment and then grunted. "Enough."

We then went into Ethan's room, a room I spent considerable time and effort expanding. Dijon peaked into Ethan's bathroom. After dismissing Ethan's space he said, "It'd be a shame for a boy to lose a room like this."

Blackie saw my body react and put his weighted hand on my shoulder.

Gordon whispered to Dijon, "It really is renovated well. It's quality construction."

Dijon ignored him. "I'd like to take a look at the backyard. I assume I can do that without your surveillance. Is that permissible Mr. Shaw?"

I reluctantly nodded my consent. Dijon and Gorman went out the sunroom door onto the backyard.

"You doing okay Jake?" Blackie asked. "You look like you want to deck the asshole and I can't say I blame you. In fact, if you don't mind, I might."

"He's one son of a bitch. I've been ready to rip him in two since he got here but I know that's not going to do me any good."

Through the sunroom's French doors, I see Dijon giving Gorman hell. "Look at that shit. Dijon doesn't seem to have any sense of humanity. He's cold Blackie. Cold."

"I know the type. Dealt with plenty of them. The way to deal with him is…ah never mind. Let's just say, I like getting into a little cruelty now and then."

I laughed. "I'll bet you do."

Dijon and Gorman walked around the backyard. Gorman might have been an architect by the way he analyzed the oversized lot, took notes and made some sketches.

Chills ran down me. My body shivered.

"What just got you Jake? And be straight with me. I saw you flinch."

I pointed to Dijon. "He has no interest in working

with me. He wants this lot, so he can tear the house and build a larger house."

"Can he do that?"

"Over my dead body or preferably his."

"I definitely choose his."

My mouth was dry. I asked Blackie, "You want something to drink?"

"Yeah, a scotch. But that can wait."

I went into the kitchen, got a glass of cold water and took a deep breath. Then Blackie said. "They're going in your office. We better go see."

I swallowed the last bit of water and headed for the door. We were in my office in a nano-second. Dijon was rifling through my desk drawers.

"What the hell, you think you're doing? Get the hell away from my desk. Your time is up. This inspection is over."

I moved toward him to grab him by his collar and throw his ass out. Gorman moved to block my path, like the little twerp thought he was a big body- guard protecting the king.

"Well, it looks like you're having a party here without me," Blackie said as he entered. "That hurts my feelings boys. And you don't want to hurt my feelings, now do you? Nah, didn't think so."

Blackie grabbed my shoulder, guided me away from Dijon and Gorman, then rifled a stare at Dijon. "But I do really like you guys, so maybe we'll get to party some other time. Yeah, I'd like that, some other time, cause now you got to go. I can tell. You're late for your next meeting." He swung his arm and gestured them the path of least resistance.

Dijon and Gorman slinked by me with Blackie pointing them toward the driveway. He turned to me and smiled. "You stay here. I'm going to show my new friends to their car."

Again, he saved me from trouble I really didn't need. I checked the draws. Everything seemed safe. I headed into the kitchen. I wanted a bourbon.

As I poured a glass, I heard. "What the hell you doing? It's not even noon. Don't start that shit." Blackie took the glass from me. "You still have to get Ethan from school." Then he belted down the booze and laughed. "But I don't."

I started laughing. "I guess it could be worse. I could have you for an enemy."

"Then you'd be in deep shit. Real deep."

"Like I'm not already?"

CHAPTER 22

She was late. She was rarely late. Impatiently I walked into the living room and through the window I saw her pull in the driveway. I went back into the kitchen and slipped on my deck shoes, then went to open the front door. By the time I got there, Camille was standing there with huge smile and bottle Pinot Noir in her hands.

"Sorry I'm late but I stopped to pick this up. I thought you might be running low."

I jokingly glanced at my watch. "Your delivery is late, and even being stunning and amazingly beautiful, there will be no tip for you young lady."

"If that's the case, then I'm going to have to take it out in trade."

"You'll have to wait until my son goes to bed before you can collect on that deal."

"That I can do. But I might need this wine in a little while."

For the next few minutes, we bantered and teased

each other but then her mood changed and I saw a serious look envelope her face. I asked, "Would you like your Pinot now?"

"No, for what I need to say, I want a clear head."

I gave myself a little space and sat in a chair across from the sofa.

"Jake, I might not get this out right because I have whirlwind of emotions going on in me."

Her face showed vulnerability. I softened and moved back over to the couch and hugged her.

"Just say any words, and if we need to, we'll fix them. How does that sound?"

"Better. Much better. Thank you. It makes me feel like we're a team again. I haven't felt that in the long time. For months I've felt you slipping further and further into your own world, a world that had no room for me. I feel that I'm doing this relationship solo. I want to know what's going on with you. No. I need to know what's going on with you. Jake, it hurts too much to do this anymore."

I hugged her again but held her a little longer.

"Camille, I'm sorry you're hurting. Hurting you is never my intention. Never. What do you need from me?"

"I just told you. I need to know what's going on. Why are you so non-present with me when we're together? That's not like you. I'm going to ask you a question and Jake, please tell me the truth. Is there someone else? Have you met someone else?"

"Honest to God Camille, that's the furthest thing from my mind. It's you and only you. Never another. Please believe that."

I was relieved to know what was bothering her. I took a breadth.

"Then what is it Jake? I need to know and I need to know now."

My chest tightened and my breath ended. I knew she deserved to know what was happening but it felt like there was a baseball in my throat blocking my words. The nerves tingled in my head, and my thoughts spun like they were in a blender. Since I met Camille, I always wanted to be her knight in shining armor riding a white stallion. But I was afraid that if I told her the truth, the knight would tumble down off his horse. I turned my head away and stared out the window.

"Damn it Jake, don't give me that shut down look. If you don't talk to me I'm leaving. Do you hear me? Damn it, talk to me?"

I wanted to speak but I was chained to my reticence. She got up and headed to the door. My body resisted moving. I let her go. The door slammed along with my heart. But then my heart yelled, "No!" I ran out the door after her. She sat in the car with her head in her hands. The engine was running. I knocked on the window.

"I'll talk. I'll talk."

She slid down the window. "What?"

"I said, I'll talk. I'll talk."

"Jake, if I go in there and you don't talk, I'm going to leave again and this time I'm not turning back. Do you understand?"

The front door slammed. "Hey what's going on here? Are you guys fighting? That's not cool."

Before I could speak, Camille said, "No Ethan, not exactly fighting. More like having a miscommunication. Go inside baby, we're fine."

"Okay. As long as you're not fighting, I'm going back in my room."

Her eyes filled with water but her face remained stern. "Jake, I'm going say this for the last time. I've had enough. If I go in the house and you clam up, withdraw and don't tell me what the hell is happening, I'm gone. Now do you understand me?"

"Yes... Loud and clear."

We went in the house and Camille sat on the couch. "Where are you going Jake?"

"In the kitchen to get a drink. You want anything?"

"No."

I poured myself a double bourbon and returned to the couch, sat down next to her and took a swig. I held silence for a minute , then walked away.

"Now where are you going?"

"Just checking on Ethan." I walked to his closed door and listened and went back to the couch. "He's playing video games. Won't be out for awhile."

"That gives you plenty of time to talk."

The baseball rose again in my throat again. After a moment of silence, from deep within my soul I murmured, "I'm scared."

"Did I hear you say you are scared? You scared? Jake Shaw scared? Scared of what? I've never seen you scared about anything. What can possibly scare you?"

I started it and I had to finish it.

"Scared that I'm not able to take care of Ethan."

"What? That's ridiculous. You're the best father I've

ever seen. What are you talking about?'

The baseball shrank, a bit. I took a sip. I stood up, shook a little and then sat back down.

"The past two years have been…well, this economy has essentially killed my business. I haven't sold a property in a year, six months, two weeks and three days. Up until now I've been living off my savings. And now I'm flat broke. There I said it, I'm flat broke."

"Jake ---"

"Let me finish while I can get it out… It actually feels good to get it off my chest. These recent months have drawn me to the wire. I recently had three deals in the pipeline. Two that looked real solid. Just those two would have got me out of this mess. But in the last couple of weeks, both of them…both of them fell through. The other one was always suspect and it proved out to be so. So I've been counting my pennies, keeping the checkbook close to my chest and using my slim credit card balances to pay what I could but now they're just about depleted. In the meantime, I've been trying to stay calm and be normal for you and Ethan. I think I've stayed good for Ethan but I haven't done well with you."

"May I say something?"

"No, not yet. There's more I want to say, while I'm still talking. I don't want to get stuck again."

Camille reached across the couch and hugged me and said, "I love you."

"I know. I know. And that's the problem."

"What does that mean?"

"Let me finish. It's the problem because I feel I let you down too…Let me finish… Camille, I love you. I love you from the bottom of my heart. I've loved only one other woman besides you and that was child's love compared to the love I have for you. I...cringe at the thought of not being able to provide for you. I know you're being patient with me. I know you want to get married. But, if I can't provide for my family, well...that's not... It rips away at me."

I couldn't look at her. I gazed out the window and felt her hand stroke my hair.

"Jake, you've been carrying this load in silence. I know this economy is hell. I'm also aware that you haven't spoken of a deal in a long time but I've had no idea the depth of your pain. You see Jake you did a good job of fooling me too, protecting me, like you did for Ethan. I just thought you were getting tired of me."

"Camille I'm sorry for that, but that's not even close to the case. The truth is, as time went on, I thought you deserved some one better than me. At least somebody solvent."

She whipped a love slap across my head.

"Now you're being stupid. There's nobody better for me, than my Jake Shaw. Nobody. Is that clear Jake Shaw? Do you understand that?"

I looked in her eyes and smiled.

"Good. Now that's clear Mr. Jake Shaw, let's get something else clear. We're a team Jake, you and me. I have some money locked away for a rainy day, and this is a rainy day."

"No way. There's no way that's going to happen. No way."

I bolted straight up and shook off the thought. I

walked into the kitchen but this time poured a glass of ice water. Camille followed me.

"Calm down Jake. Calm down. I get it. I get it. I understand. Breathe."

I drank the water and emotionally withdrew.

"Now, don't withdraw from me. This meeting is not over. Don't stop talking to me. If you let me, I'm in this with you. I'm in it with you."

We went back to the couch.

"There's good news here too Jake."

"Then please let me know what it is, cause I can't find it."

"No matter what's happening in this hellish real estate market, you still have your house."

Her words ripped through my gut. "If I do, I might have it only for a little while longer."

"What do you mean?"

"I'm going to be three months late in paying my mortgage to Mangello."

"I know Mangello. He's your friend, He'll work with you and in a short time ---"

I raised my hand to stop her.

"If Mangello could help me he would. But he can't. His back is up against the wall financially and he's got to sell the mortgage on this house. There's no other way for him. We talked and I understand."

"Well, when he sells the paper, you'll just pay the new holder. I'm sure you can negotiate for a little time until this market turns around and you can make some money. And then you just catch up."

"First, I wish it were that simple. The truth is this market is not going to turn quickly. I spoke with

Robert Munroe and he and his cronies see this market flat, if not dead for an undetermined time. And I don't have a single prospect."

"And second?"

"And second, Mangello had three prospects to buy the paper but now he's down to one."

"One is better than none."

"Maybe not in this case."

"Why do say that?"

"Because the guy he has left is trouble. Nasty trouble."

"How can you say that? Have you met him?"

"More than met him. I almost physically threw his ass out of here twice, the arrogant bastard. He's a pompous Frenchman named Dijon."

The color went out of Camille's face. She looked faint.

"Camille, Camille are you alright? Can I get you some water? Something else?"

She took a deep breath, wiped her face with her hand and sighed deeply. Then she bent over, put her face in her hands and began to cry. "Get me the Pinot, large glass," she sobbed.

I hustled into the kitchen, popped the cork from the bottle she bought and brought a glass and the bottle back to her. I filled half the glass and gave it to her. She stopped crying, inhaled the aroma of the wine, and took a drink. Her face was red and wet.

"You did say Dijon, didn't you? Napoleon Dijon?"

"I don't know about Napoleon? I think he used Leon."

She bit her lip and said, "That's him. Napoleon

Dijon. He shortens it to Leon. But Napoleon fits his personality better."

"Do you know Dijon?"

She took a longer drink of the wine, put the empty glass on the coffee table and slunk down into the couch.

"Camille do you know this jerk?"

The bottom fell out of my stomach. What the hell is going on?

"Do you know this guy?"

"Yes, I know him. More than I'd like to admit."

Confusion rambled my brain.

"Let me explain, " she said.

"I'm listening," I said trying to be calm.

She straightened up and reached for the bottle of wine and then pulled back.

"It was before I met you. I went to an art function downtown. I was doing the usual mix and mingle routine, when Hillary Brooks walked over with Dijon and introduced me to him. His first words were, 'Il est agreeable de vous recontrer.'"

"What does that mean?"

"It wasn't what he said but how he said it. It was first time I ever heard native French in Sarasota. It just means, 'It's delightful to meet you.'"

"And?"

"We spoke French the rest of the night. He was charming and astute is his appreciation of art. The evening went fast and when the lights were dimming to signal the end of the evening, he asked me if I wanted to go for a drink and continue with our French conversation. I thanked him for that opportunity but declined. However, I did offer the possibility of lunch at the C'est La Vie. He immediately accepted. We made a date and I left for the evening. He offered to walk me to my car but again, I declined."

"And…?"

"When I got to the C'est La Vie, Dijon was sitting with a group of women, talking English with a heavy French accent, pouring on the charm. But when he saw me he excused himself abruptly and focused his attention solely on me."

"Smart man."

"As usual the food was excellent and Jerome, the waiter was a dear. We ordered in French and even though I have eaten in C'est La Vie many times, I felt like I was back home in Nice. It was a touching experience. I learned he grew up in Marseilles, which is about a hundred miles from Nice. During lunch we talked art and of course, discussed the French impressionists Cezanne, Renoir, Monet. It was delightful but… but, there was something about him that I didn't trust. I wasn't exactly sure what was, so I had my wall up."

I sipped my bourbon and she matched me with wine.

"So when we finished lunch he asked me out a regular date."

"Like a date, date?"

"Yes, a date, date. But I said for right now, I'd be comfortable with another lunch. And that was certainly true. I enjoyed talking about France, the good, the beautiful and the romantic. It brought back home to me. I didn't realize I missed it until we talked about it."

"What did he say?"

"Oh, he turned on the charm and tried to persuade me. I felt like I was prey to a hungry lion."

"So?"

"So a week later, I had my second lunch with him at C'est La Vie. This time he was at his most charming. Still speaking not a word of English, all French. He told me that he never met anyone like me. That he thought I was the most beautiful woman he's ever seen. He believed that we are destiny's couple. Essentially, he spent the whole lunch charming me, persuading me to go to dinner with him."

"A persistent bastard."

"You have no idea."

"Don't tell me you went to dinner with him."

She re-filled her glass. I emptied mine.

"No I didn't but during the week prior to the third lunch, I did a little asking around about Napoleon Dijon."

"And…?"

"My instincts were right. He was the ultimate player. Suave, charming, intelligent, successful and totally self-centered."

"So?"

"So at lunch I again politely declined dinner. Once he realized that he wasn't getting what he wanted, his colors changed. He became obnoxious and rude. But mind you in French, so to everyone else in the restaurant it sounded well, French. Then he caught himself being rude and turned the charm back on. But when he saw I was on to him, he became even ruder. So I got up and walked out the restaurant and hurried to my car. Half way there, I turned around to see him walking fast toward me. I made it to my car and drove away as fast as I could."

"Good. Then you were done with this asshole."

" That's what I thought but not even close. "

"What…?'

"Jake, it was just the beginning."

I was getting ready to make this guy some concrete shoes and take him for a boat ride.

"What's the rest?"

"He found out where I lived. That's when I lived in the little house on Oak Street. He regularly sent me flowers, which I refused to accept. Cards that I returned to sender. He left me messages on my voice mail, professing his undying love. In short he badgered, stalked me so much I took out a restraining order on him. He told people I was the one who got away, he'd never forget me and that I would eventually succumb to his pursuit. And overtime I found out more about him, including that he was crazy, ruthless and a sleaze in his business dealings."

"The same song for different dances."

By then she was crying again and I'm more than pissed.

"Jake, I never, ever did anything to encourage him. Never. I had hoped he'd go away and I thought he did But now this Jake, I brought him to you. He's followed me to you. It's my fault. I am so sorry, so sorry. I brought my nightmare into your home."

I took her in my arms, stroked her head and rubbed her tears away.

"Camille, a little while ago, you said we are a team, you and me. I don't know how, but I promise you... promise you, this nightmare is going to end for the both of us. And I keep my promises."

She sunk into my chest and I vowed to myself to do whatever was necessary to take care of this mess. Whatever it took.

CHAPTER 23

It was no big deal, so I thought. The table was empty, so I sat down. The patrons at Moe's Place looked at me like I'm crazy. They sensed trouble. One person whispered to another and heads shook in confusion, followed by mumbling. I sure didn't want trouble.

A waitress I didn't recognize came over to the table and bluntly asked, "You're waiting for Blackie right?"

"That's right. Can I have a decaf?"

She smiled gave a thumbs up sign. "Coming right up." Thankfully the protective patronage piped down.

Then I realized what was going on. The cast of characters who frequented Moe's Place got their panties in a twist because I took Blackie's table, but when they were assured I would be with Blackie, I was good to sit and have my coffee in peace. Talk about protective and territorial.

My stomach was unsettled, food was not of interest. There were too many things on my mind to eat. Louie was expecting my first delivery. I told him I had my eye on a silver Aston Martin and that it would vanish from Sarasota that night. With a sticker value close to three hundred grand, my fee would be substantial. When I imagined the money, it felt really good. I could visualize some of my bills getting paid, including maybe getting Mangello out of his hole. Yeah, it felt real good. But when the waitress brought my coffee, I sank back into reality and the thought of the cost of getting caught and it turned my stomach even more. Getting caught would surely turn life upside down. But it was a chance I needed to take. In the past, it was a quick ride to the bank. I assured myself, this time it would be the same. No big deal. Just like old times. If… I was lucky.

"Hey buddy boy, this table is reserved."

"So I noticed from the looks I got when I sat down. I'm glad somebody remembered me."

"They're just watching out for me. Bunch a good guys."

The waitress brought Blackie his morning java, hot and black.

"Say Jake my boy, did you see my Yankees yesterday? They slammed the hell out of Boston. Beat'em 12 to 1. Now that makes me smile."

"I'll bet it does."

Then Blackie's face went sour. "But, I'll tell you what doesn't make me smile, that French dude at your house. He's no good. He has a stench to him. Real bad."

He took a gulp of coffee . "I never told you this but I have a good smeller. In fact it's the best smeller in the business. True, only a few guys can do it but I sure as hell can. I can smell an odor of trouble on some people. You know when a beautiful woman walks by, even if she's not wearing perfume, I can just smell her femininity. It smells delicious. Well, this guy smells like cat piss."

I laughed. Blackie was many things including funny. Sadly, I knew he was right.

"As far as I'm concerned your nose is on the right trail. And, I'll tell you why?"

"Hold on, I need to get some food. You eating?"

"Not hungry right now."

Blackie gave his order to the waitress and said. "Go ahead. Tell me about this cat piss."

After I told him about Camille's s experience with Dijon, Blackie's head moved in a reptilian motion. Some deep, instinctive and protective cord had been struck. He squinted, and gazed off, as if to a distant place and time. A few minutes later, he took a deep breath and re-entered the here and now.

He said. "I'm going to do a little asking and looking around about this guy. What's his name again?"

"Dijon. Napoleon Dijon."

"Napoleon Dijon. Napoleon eh?"

"He goes by Leon."

"Napoleon eh," he repeated.

"What you looking for?"

"An enzymatic remover. It works on cat piss."

"A what remover?"

"Enzymatic remover. It's the best thing for taking care of cat piss."

"Find it quick. The quicker the better."

The conversation switched back to the Yankees. He

ate his breakfast. I nursed my coffee. Then it was time for me to leave.

"Listen I've got some things to handle and want to thank you for watching Ethan tonight, so I can hopefully do some business with my investor from Tampa."

"No worries. I love the kid almost as I love my own."

"Even though I need to leave you alone right now, I know you're in safe hands with your posse in this place," I joked.

He laughed, turned his head toward the eclectic group on the other side of the restaurant. "They do look out for me... Moe's Place is a good place."

***

I got to my car and immediately dialed Mangello.

"Hello Frank. How's the day treating you?"

"To be honest Jake, not good. So please give me some good news."

"Actually, I might have some."

"I'm listening."

"I have a long time investor in Tampa, who's anxious to pick up some properties on the cheap. He's a flush cash buyer, so closings would be quick and easy. So, I'm asking if you can back this guy Dijon off a bit, give me a little time to work this thing out. Make us both right."

"Jake, I'm happy for you; hope it pays off for you. But, I have to go where the cash is and until this investor of yours starts buying and closing properties, you don't have any cash. And to make matters worse for you but better for me, Dijon is pushing me to close as quickly as I can, so I'm trying to get things in order. My attorney is out of town, so I need to wait until next week to see when this will get done. So you don't have much time."

"Frank, we've had a good relationship. I just ask for as much time as you can give me. This Dijon is bad news."

"Yeah Jake, I see that, and I'm sorry it's got to be him but his cash is green, even if it's not so clean."

"Frank, I'll be back to you in a few days. Just keep me in mind when dealing with him. Okay?"

"I'll do my best Jake. But not promising anything."

I hung up and drove home quickly. I wanted to be home, like a guard at the fort.

***

"Ethan, Blackie will be here any minute. Are you ready?"

"Just about dad. Can't decide which Rays hat to wear."

"Where the one that fits you."

"You're funny dad, there all adjustable."

There was a knock at the door.

"Ethan, Blackie's here, decide quickly. I'll get the door."

The front door swung open and I heard Blackie. "Hellooo Zorro!"

"Zorro? What do you mean?" I asked.

"You're dressed like Zorro man, all in black. Black

jeans, black tone on tone shirt, black shoes, black belt. Where's your black mask?"

"I didn't realize I did that." I lied. "Must be my mood. Like the dreary weather."

"Not a cheery way to meet a client, Zorro."

"I get your point but it's too late to change."

"New cologne?" Blackie asked.

"I don't wear cologne."

"New soap?"

"What's your point here?"

"You just smell different buddy boy. You smell different."

"Must be the shampoo. New shampoo."

"That's got to be it. My suggestion is…change it. It stinks."

Ethan ran into the living room and pounced on Blackie.

"Don't hurt him Ethan he's fragile. And, give me a hug. I got to go to work. See you guys later. You might be in bed when I get home, so give me an extra hug."

"I'll give you one of my super hugs." And he gave me a hug, a hug I hoped to feel again.

***

It was 7:02 p.m. when I parked the Highlander in a dark spot in the parking lot of a popular restaurant. I put on a pair of black running shoes and a black baseball cap and grabbed my magical tools. I felt like I was in a movie. I walked two blocks to a three-story medical office building with the open parking area underneath. It was there the beautiful silver Aston

Martin was parked, where it's always parked Monday thru Thursday evenings. It was waiting for me to take it for a ride. I've admired its beauty many times before when I passed on my way to the sports bar. I ambled past the building and surveyed the area. My sense was the Aston Martin must belong to a young stud surgeon. I breathed deeply, trying to calm my fear and to block out any morality, as well. I had to. There was no room for either in this situation. I needed to focus on the take and not the danger of getting caught or the consequences of failure. There was no room for failure. My body quivered with the truth, reminding me that I wasn't the man I used to be. But I needed to forget that. I was out of options. I had to do it. In minutes, it would be over and I'd be driving free, on my way to Tampa and my payoff.

I sat on a street bench in front of the building, observed the environment and stalked the car. My heart pounded, my head whirled, my breath went shallow and my hands were moist. It wasn't like this before. When I felt it was good to go, I moved toward the car. My legs shook as I got near the prize. A moment later, I heard a building door open and I heard voices coming toward me. I quickly ducked down behind a Mercedes. My heart wanted to jump out of my chest. Two guys headed directly for the Aston Martin. One of them hit the key fob and unlocked it. They were laughing. I was scared. Without suspecting my presence, they got in and drove away. I sat in a sweating lump. After a couple of minutes, my heart slowed down and my breath came back. I checked out the area. I was still alone. I got up and tried to calmly walk away from the area and not burst into a full sprint.

I got back to the Highlander, jumped in, and closed the door. Zorro escaped disaster. It was a close call, too close. Life, as I knew it, could have been over... damn. I needed a drink, more than one. My favorite sports bar was near. But in my Zorro outfit? I decided against it. It would be better to go home.

***

In five minutes I was home. Alone. Safe. I poured a shot of bourbon. It felt great going done. I poured another. Then I heard a car pull into the driveway. Was I followed? The front door opened.

"Hey buddy boy, I thought you'd be back later tonight. What happened?"

"I was on the highway and got a call. They had some kind of emergency and needed to re-schedule. Just got here and poured a bourbon. Want one?"

"No thanks. Got me a six pack."

"Yeah dad, I got me a six-pack too. I need some cold beer with my pizza you know."

"I'll give you cold beer alright. I'll pour it right over your head."

Blackie rapped his beer in his arm like he was protecting a football.

"Don't go wasting my beer, either of you," Blackie says with a laugh.

"That pizza looks and smells good. Got a piece of that for me?" I asked.

"We sure do buddy boy. We got an extra-large. Dig

in."

After the three of us quickly killed the pizza, Ethan went to his room to play a video game.

"You know, I love that kid like he's my own but it's bitter sweet hanging out with him. It makes me want to be with Bobby so bad." Blackie said.

"I can't imagine what you're feeling and I don't want to."

"Some nights, I just want to jump in my truck and head north. There's not a lot holding me here, except for the weather in the winter… and oh yeah…you two. Well, Ethan anyway, maybe not you."

"Sounds like you're getting close to leaving."

"Like I told you at Ethan's game, the owner of my condo likes having an ex-cop around, so I have no lease. Most of the furniture, I'd give to Goodwill. The rest of my stuff will fit in a small u-haul on the back of my truck. I can be gone in no time. Just got to make the decision."

"What will I do without you around here?"

"Screw you, you don't even cook for me. Or root for the Yankees."

"I guess the good news would be, there'd be less wear and tear on the couch. And for sure fewer beer bottles to throw out. Come to think of it, sounds like good idea, when you leaving?"

Blackie rubbed his right eye with his fist. "Now you hurt my feelings."

"Poor baby. Have another brewski."

It was around ten o'clock when I called Louie to tell him what happened with the Aston Martin. He understood and was glad I escaped trouble and encouraged me to try it again. He said it was just part of the business.

I fell into bed, took a deep breath and let my body relax. The clean sheets never felt better and the pillow never softer. Ethan was in his room, safe. It could've been over tonight. History. My lungs emptied with relief, my eyes watered with gratitude and my mind started to slow down until I thought of that rodent Dijon. I still had to deal with him. I tried to sleep but that wasn't happening. After a half- hour, I got up and headed into the garage, put the gloves on and started to dance with Henry.

CHAPTER 24

By the time I got to the park the fog had blanketed the small peninsula and it had begun to rain. To my surprise, I saw Odin coming from around the curve. He was just finishing his walk. I waved as he approached me.

"Jake, I'm surprised to see you in this soup."

"And I'm more surprised to see you finished already."

"I decided to get my walk in early to avoid the rain. If you want to talk, let's go over to O'Learys and sit under the roof."

"Good idea."

O'Learys Tiki Hut was a bayside restaurant and bar on the edge of the park. We sat at a picnic table near the water; the fog was so thick, we could barely see the bay. Not surprisingly, we were the only people there.

"Before you ask me, yes I did my homework. So I'm ready to go. What are we going to talk about today?

"Your awakened imagination."

"My what?"

"Your awakened imagination.

I laughed a bit. "Okay, I'm listening."

"Actually it's funnier to think about your sleeping imagination because that's what most imaginations are doing, sleeping. And that includes yours Jake."

"Okay. You've got my attention."

"Remember we talked about that we are all expressions of Spirit, that we are Onederful?"

"Yes, of course."

"Well our imagination is a gift from Source, it's the creative tool we can use to consciously express Spirit's power through us. As Source's creative power sparked the big bang, you can use your awakened imagination to spark your own life, take charge of it and have dominion over it."

"Now you really got my interest."

"Albert Einstein, the brilliant physicist, knew the power of the imagination and stated its importance succinctly when he said, 'Imagination is more important than knowledge.'"

"Why is that?"

"This is not taking anything away from the value of knowledge but knowledge is derived from the past, lives in the present and has no creative power. The imagination has the creative power of Spirit and because of this holds the potential future. Knowledge is where we come from, where we are, while the imagination is where we are going."

"I never thought of it like that."

"Everything we see in the world; the buildings, the cars, clothes, whatever, some person first imagined.

As kids we were well connected to our imagination but as we got older we were told and learned to, 'stop imagining things.' In essence, we're told to stop using the creative power of Source and follow the well-worn path of the human way like everyone else."

"Isn't using your imagination just pretending?"

"It isn't just pretending. It's using the creative power of Source's within you to write the future you desire. Analyze the word pretend, pre-tend. Pre is a prefix that means before. Tend means to work, like in a garden. So before you work, you give thought to what you want to grow in your garden. Right?"

"Right."

"So you pretend your garden, which takes place in your imagination, your awakened imagination. It's awakened because you are consciously aware, choosing mindfully what you want to harvest. And you need to practice using your awakened imagination and not your sleeping imagination."

"What's my sleeping imagination?"

"Do you ever worry about the situation you are in and what's going to happen?"

"What me worry? Of course I do. Far too much. Don't we all?"

"Worry is the pretending of a sleeping imagination. We never choose to worry, it just happens unconsciously. How does it feel when you worry?"

"Horrible. My stomach can get in knots, sometimes my head feels like its spinning. Other times it feels like my blood is boiling."

"So there's emotion?"

"Yeah. Plenty of it."

"In essence when you're worrying you are imagining, pretending, a future you don't want. And since your imagination holds the creative power of Spirit, you are expressing a bleak future and feeling horrible in the present. Not to mention how you'll feel in the future."

"Damn, that's what I do alright."

"Yes. It's like going into your garden and instead of watering the flowers, you're watering the weeds. Does it make sense to water weeds?"

"Hell no!"

"Here's another way to look at it.

"I'm listening."

"Think of your life as a movie."

"Okay, I like movies."

"Let's call it, 'Jake's Movie.'"

"Sounds good to me.

"Every movie needs a writer, a lead actor, a director. In your movie, you are the writer and the actor."

"Who is the director?"

"We'll get to that later."

"Okay."

"As the writer, your job is not to write the entire script. Your job is simply to write the happing ending. In your current financial situation, what would be your happy ending?"

"That's easy. I want the money to pay all my bills, I want my son safe and secure in our home, I want Dijon out of my life and Camille's life and I want my business to be successful."

"Then as the writer, it's your job to use your imagination and write a scene that depicts such a joyous occasion. That's your happy ending. Then your job as an actor is to imaginatively pretend that scene. Rehearse your part in that scene in your imagination. See yourself in that scene joyously celebrating your happy ending. And Jake."

"Yes?"

"Remember what you said about worry, how horrible it feels."

"It sucks."

"Emotions have power and are vitally important in the playing of your role for you to have your happing ending. As any good actor does in a movie, bring the emotions to the role. Jake, feel what you'd feel in that happing ending. Practice it. Rehearse it over and over and until it's palpable to you. Emote Jake. Emote. Feel it like it's already been done because on the unseen level Jake, it has been done."

"Odin, as you were talking I felt utter relief. I felt a load fall from my chest."

"That's what most people feel first, relief. Relief from the stress and pressure of their situation, no matter what their happy ending is, no matter what the issue. After relief, other more joyous feelings arise."

"That actually feels so much better already… just imagining my happy ending. "

"That's good Jake, because you're starting to experience the future you want. You're pretending it."

"Odin, what about the director? Who directs?"

"Your Higher Power, the same Source intelligence that sparked and sustains the universe, is the director. You might say, the ultimate director. Remember the power of Source comes through you. You Jake are not the power. You're the channel and expression of that power. So you write your script, and your Higher Power directs your scripts. Your Higher Power arranges the plot and organizes all the details to fulfill your happy ending. It's not your job to figure out how your Higher Power will do that. Actually it's way beyond your pay grade."

"My job then is to write my happing ending and as the actor my job is to pretend, rehearse my happing ending in my imagination and feel the scene as if it was real, as if I was actually experiencing it."

"That's right."

"That's it?"

"And, as the actor actually follow any intuitive directions you get from your Higher Power director. If you feel impelled to do a particular thing, do it. Follow your inner guidance."

"And other than that, just wait?"

"And trust. Trust your Higher Power to arrange the plot to arrive at your happing ending. Realize, the necessary plot arrangements are happening behind the scenes by Spirit. Sort of like off camera."

"Odin this seems silly, too simple to be true, never mind actually work."

"It's not silly, it's truly profound and frankly it is simple, but you must apply yourself or else nothing happens. You as the writer of the movie have to believe in your relationship with the director and in the director's ability to do the job or else you won't get your happy ending. Realize Jake, this process is a metaphysical law of the universe, which was known to the ancient mystics, and written in the sacred books, 'first in the unseen; then in the seen.'

As we evolve, we begin to awaken to our true nature as spiritual beings having this human experience, as the living expressions of Source. Jake don't just take my word for it, prove it to your self. Work with it. Test it. Make it work for you."

"Sounds like I can have heaven on earth, if it works."

"It works Jake. It works. The more you're connected to Spirit within you, the more creative power will pulsate through you to provide many happy endings. Cultivate your Onederful relationship and experience what happens."

"Anything else?"

"One last thing. Here's a brief mantra I use to keep me on track. It's simply, 'Thank you. Thank you. Thank you.'"

"Thank you. Thank you. Thank you," I repeated.

"Yes. The first 'thank you' is to Source for its Presence. The second 'thank you' is for Source being the essence of your life and your Onederful relationship. The third 'thank you' is to Source for the amazing power of its expression within you through your awakened imagination. Thank you. Thank you. Thank you."

We sat in silence for about ten minutes and I watched the fog lift, the sky begin to clear, and the sun peek out from behind the clouds.

"Jake, your homework is simple. Write your happing ending and rehearse your role."

I smiled at the old man and said. "Thank you. Thank you. Thank you." And I truly meant it.

CHAPTER 25

"Dad look! Alligators! Lots of them," Ethan said with excitement.

He was right. At least a dozen alligators were sunning themselves on the bank across the river.

"I like this place. What's it called again?"

"Myakka River State Park."

"How big is it?"

"It's big. According to this pamphlet it's 37,000 acres."

"Wow! I don't know what that means but I know it means big."

" There are lots of things to do here. We can canoe, take a boat tour or hike some trails or ---"

"I know what I want," he exclaimed. "I want to get closer to those alligators."

"Hold on there tiger, it's best they're on the other side of the river. You don't want to tempt them. They're big fellas and if they're hungry, you'd be like an Oreo cookie to them. One sweet bite."

He walked along the huge pipe laying across river leading toward the resting gators. He got to the middle of the pipe and stopped.

"Good idea to stop. No crossing to the other side." I said.

"I just wish I could get real close."

"I'm sure you do."

He looked down along the bank on our side of the river.

"Maybe I can get closer if I go down there and look straight across at them."

Our side of the river appeared safe enough. The river seemed wide enough to give protection.

"That's okay. Just be careful."

I followed behind him allowing him his freedom but with an invisible rope of caution around him. He shuffled down the bank directly across the river from the group of gators. He was getting a good look at them and they were getting a good look at him. After a couple of minutes, a patch of tall grass near him moved and… I saw it. It was huge.

"Ethan, stand perfectly still." I said with authority but without wanting to panic him. "Listen to me carefully. Don't move an inch buddy. There's a gator in the grass about twenty feet from you. Stay still and do not move. I'm coming to get you. I'm going to walk slowly toward you until I get to you. Then I'm going pick you up and run as fast as I can to that observation deck. However…however if I say run, you run as fast as you can and go straight to the deck. Go straight, don't zig zag. I repeat don't zig-zag and don't stop running until you get there. Do you understand?"

Fright covered his face, as adrenalin shot through my body.

"Yes sir."

"This will be over before you know it. Just be still."

With my eyes locked on the gator, I took slow, easy steps as my heart raced. I had no intention of startling the big gator. Step by easy, fluid step. Suddenly, the gator moved slightly to the left... but didn't advance. Then out of the corner of my eye I saw two gators on the other the bank enter the water and come in our direction. My heart jumped. As fast as I could run, I grabbed Ethan, lifted him onto my shoulders and ran like an Olympic sprinter toward the deck. The startled gator darted after us, but soon stopped when he realized he'd never catch us. We reached the deck with all our limbs and body parts in place. I put Ethan gently down on the bench and crumbled down next to him. My lungs were burning, my breath lost and my legs shaking. He grabbed me, hugged me and didn't let go.

"I never knew you could run so fast," he said astonished.

"I never have. Ever. Are you alright?"

"Yes sir."

I glanced back to where we left the gator. He had moved up in our direction and with him were the two other gators. Thank God I'd been running more consistently. Thank God.

After a few minutes of holding me, he let go. And like any resilient kid, he was ready for his next adventure.

"Can we take one of those boat rides?"

My breath and heart rate were back to normal but my legs were still shaking. "I need something to drink." I said.

"Okay, how about we get a coke and maybe a candy bar or something else good. And then we can check out the boat rides."

"After what we've been through, you deserve anything you want."

We rested on a bench by the park's concession store, drinking cokes and munching on Baby Ruth candy bars. I enjoyed the safety and the calm of the moment. It felt primitively peaceful.

"Dad, was my mom cool like Camille?"

His question surprised me. He hadn't asked about his mom in years. My mind hustled for an answer.

"Ethan, we are all different in our own unique way. And yes, your mom was cool. She was very cool too."

"Cause Camille is really cool," he emphasized.

"You are right buddy, Camille is really cool."

"If mom was cool and Camille is cool, why don't you marry Camille like you did mom?"

First the gator, now that question. The day was not boring.

"Ethan that's a real good question. And it's somewhat complicated, would you mind if I give it some thought before I answer it?"

"That's okay. I was just thinking what it would be like to have Camille for my mom and it would be definitely cool."

It was a discussion I wanted to get away from as fast I did the gator. I asked. "Let's go check out the boat ride. Maybe it's getting time for them to leave on another trip. Do you have to go to the bathroom before we go?"

"Yeah man. I mean, yes sir. But I can go by myself."

"Okay big guy, the men's room is right over there."

The boat ride on the calm Myakka River gave me time to regroup from Ethan's question. The reason was obvious why I didn't marry Camille. Not with my financial battles raging. That would have been like asking her to join me among the alligators.

***

6 p.m. Ethan, Camille and I were in the kitchen getting ready for dinner. Ethan was setting the table. I was cutting the vegetables and Camille was orchestrating the entire meal. Sometimes out of the mouth of a kid comes the obvious observation. Ethan's question from the afternoon still had hold of my mind. It had changed the way I looked at Camille. Was my financial situation the only reason I was holding back from marrying Camille?

At dinner Ethan bolted down his food and headed to his room to play video games. Camille and I continued to eat slowly.

"So how is Jake Shaw tonight?"

"He is with the most wonderful woman in the world, so I'd say he is doing super."

"Thank you for the delightful compliment, which I gladly accept, but how is Jake Shaw really doing tonight? And this time I'd like an authentic answer."

"Man, you're like an x-ray machine that can cut

through all the crap." I laughed.

"And, you're like a butterfly trying to escape the net. Tell me the truth."

"The authentic truth, deep from my bones is…Jake Shaw could be better. He has a lot on his plate and he's doing the best he can with it."

"I'm sure you'll clear up your plate, like you cleared Ethan away from that alligator. Is there anything I can do to help you clear it up?"

"You do it ever day by just being you. Your smile raises the altitude of my attitude. However, come to think about it there is something you can do."

"Anything, just tell me."

"After Ethan goes to sleep, you might tend to my yearning body."

"Jake Shaw, you are such a guy," she said laughing at me. "Honestly is there anything else I can do for you?"

"Honestly babe, I have no earthly idea. Just be you and love me like you do."

"That's easy."

"Good. That's all I need right now."

CHAPTER 26

"Where the hell you been? I've already been here an hour." Blackie was already chewing down on a bagel. Moe's Place was packed.

"Fat chance detective, you're only on the first page of the sports section. Not even in the box scores yet. Your cook must have had the morning off, so you got here early to fill that hole in your sizeable stomach."

"You should have been a cop."

"No chance of that either, no chance at all."

The waitress refilled Blackie's coffee and poured me a cup of decaf. Blackie ordered a forklift of pancakes and then scowled out the window at the parking lot like he was waiting for trouble.

"What are you checking out detective? Expecting somebody?"

"Yeah, you got that right." He turned to me with a serious look on his face. "Buddy boy, you're being tailed."

I took a quick look out the window, "Where?

Who?"

"Camille too."

"You're kidding?"

"This ain't no joke. Your story about Camille's history with Dijon, smelled sour to me, so I did a little detective work and also had each of you followed. For the record, my smeller still works good. What my associate discovered was you're both being tailed. So we tailed your tailer, who led us back to Dijon."

"I'm going to find that son of bitch and ---"

"Hold on tiger. Hold on. There's not much we can do about it right now. Can't prove anything's wrong."

"This guy is a viper I want to step on."

"He's a viper more than you know. You're not the only guy that has reason to step on him. There's a line of them."

"What can I do?"

"For now sit tight and pay attention to your surroundings. This isn't a twenty-four hour surveillance gig they're doing. It's more like a small reconnaissance assignment. I think it has more to do Dijon's fixation with Camille. Crushing you is his sick way of revenge. And believe me this dude is a sicko."

"It pisses me off. The whole situation pisses me off."

The waitress arrived with food. Blackie dove into his pancakes. I sipped my decaf. My stomach was in knots.

"If you only had the money to pay off your mortgage you might be done with this guy. Maybe, maybe not."

I took a few moments and stabilized my breath and got my anger a little more controlled.

"I'm working on a few things. One that I didn't tell

you about."

"Jake, you holding out on me?"

"Hardly. I've been meeting with an old man who's explaining some metaphysical, spiritual principles to me so I can possibly use them to change my situation and my life."

"Meta what? What principles? What are you talking about? Buddy boy, don't give me that load, that shit is crazy making. Work is the answer, not that metaphysical crap. That's for sure."

"Sounds like you've got a strong opinion of that."

"I sure do buddy boy. With all the shit going on in the world, what we need to do is to take business in our own hands, right here, right now.

"I hear you. I'm not saying I bought into to it."

"Through the years, I seen bad guys and good guys and the bad won a lot of the time. I learned the best thing you can do is handle your business right here and the sooner the better. That includes the justice system buddy boy and the philosophical crap you're talking about. No sir, that aint my way."

I needed some mind space and headed to the men's room. When I came back, I changed the subject.

"Before I forget, any chance you can watch Ethan tonight? My Tampa clients called me this morning and asked if I can meet with them tonight."

"Are they going to show this time?"

"I'm counting on it."

Blackie had cooled down. "Sure no problem."

"Thanks. I won't be late. It helps me a lot."

"Tampa clients eh? Both times you mentioned these Tampa clients, I get a sense of trouble. Something just don't smell right. When I was back on the job when something smelled fishy, it usually was and eventually the fish showed up floating on the top of the water. Be careful with those guys, you already got enough trouble."

"I'll watch my back, but these guys are just finance geeks."

"Finance geeks, who smell bad."

***

7:00 p.m. I drove slowly past the medical building and spotted the Aston Martin parked under the building with only one other car, three spaces away. My hands began to sweat and my heart beat faster. I continued to drive two blocks and parked in a near full restaurant lot. I slipped off my white shirt and put on a black one. I changed from shoes to black sneakers. I took a long breadth and tried to get centered. Blackie's words about a dead fish floating on the top, floated in my head. I knew what I was going to do was wrong on many levels and at the very least this guy didn't deserve his car to be stolen.

If I pulled this off without a hitch, I'd get in deeper with Louie and his organization. Did I really want that? There was no way to really win tonight but two big ways to lose. I knew I just had to roll the dice.

I sat on the street bench scoping out the environment, with an eye on the target. My thoughts however, were on Odin's words. I didn't know if he was right but my sense was he wasn't wrong. But what I did know for sure was that stealing this car was not something to be proud of doing. It was not something I'd want Ethan to know about, nor Camille. But I did want to keep a roof over Ethan's head and I wanted it to be the roof we had.

Then for a moment, I had a quick thought about not doing it and I relaxed. However, it was short lived. When I envisioned Dijon laughing at me, fire rose through my body and it overrode all the good within me. I had no other choice. I needed the money and I needed it immediately. I wasn't going to let that rodent win. I needed to protect Ethan and keep Camille far from Dijon.

I nonchalantly walked to the medical building, my tool bag in my hand, repeating to myself, 'I need to do this. I need to do this. This will be easy. This will be easy. I have the money. I have the money.' There it was, parked alone, my ticket to a payday. Without a second's thought I approached the car directly. I was twenty feet from the car, feeling in the bag for the opener when a door slammed and I heard someone walking. I ducked behind a building column. It was the young doctor, who owned the car. He scared the hell out of me. I couldn't believe it. For the second time I was almost caught. I dried my hands off on my pants.

He unlocked the car door and grabbed something off the seat. His cell phone rang. He fumbled for his phone in his pants pocket.

"Hi babe, what's up?" He said and then listened to his caller for a moment. "Tell you what, I have about an hour's worth of work left to do then I'll get you and we'll go out and grab a bite to eat. Sound good? ...

Great, see you real soon…Love you too."

He shut the door but I didn't see or hear him lock it. He walked away and I heard the building door slam shut. I was alone with an unlocked Aston Martin waiting for me to take it for a ride. This would be easy. A piece of cake. Money in my hands.

But I couldn't move. My body felt like it was cast in concrete while the voice inside me yelled…. "You know better than this." There had to be another way, a better way, a right way. My inner resistance was firm. I couldn't do it. Wouldn't do it…I didn't do it.

The hell with Dijon.

CHAPTER 27

The next morning at 9:40 a.m. I sat in my car in the parking lot of Villani Enterprises in Tampa. My decision not to take the Aston Martin essentially cancelled my deal with Louie. I wanted to tell him face-to-face, man-to-man. That is if RH hadn't already told him that I didn't come across with the goods. I didn't want him to be wondering what happened. But first I needed to call Camille.

I grabbed my phone and hit her number.

"Hey babe, how you doing today?" I asked.

"I'll be doing fine when this cloud cover lifts. I wanted to work outside on a landscape painting I have a small commission to do. And I need the sunshine."

"Give it time, the sun always rises and shines in sunny Sarasota. Listen. I've got a lot on my plate right now, so how about if we take a rain check on tonight?"

"Here's the deal lover boy. If there's a lot on your plate, then we'll both have to clean it because there's no way we're rain checking our connection tonight."

Her surety, though not what I expected to hear, felt good. "I hear you loud and clear. See you at six."

"Yes you will. Count on it."

I had changed my mind about meeting with Camille. That was easy. But I wasn't going to change my mind about dealing with Louie and that wouldn't be easy. I gave a lot thought on how best to do it but I still didn't know exactly how I was going to tell him. It would've been nice if I could just say that I changed my mind, shake hands and walk away. But there was no way it was going to be that easy, especially with that guy Joe Bell aware of what's going on. I just needed to trust that whatever was going to happen, was the responsibility of my director and geared toward my happy ending.

I entered the lobby of the building. It was empty. There was no beautiful Ms. Roma to greet me. I sat down on the couch, and picked up a copy of the Dupont Registry and leafed through its pages of exotic cars. Fifteen minutes later the elevator door opened and out pranced Ms. Roma. The moment she spotted me, her posture went from relaxed to formal.

"Mr. Shaw how nice to see you. How can I help you?"

"I need to see Mr. Villani. And…he's not expecting to see me."

"I'm sure he's not expecting you and you can't see him."

I don't know how long she's worked for Louie but she was a fierce gate-keeper.

"I'm sure if Mr. Villani knows I'm here, he'll see me."

"That might be perfectly true, however, you can

only see him if he's here and he's not."

"I see." I checked out the time, 10:15. He must be running late. "I can wait."

"Suit yourself. It's going to be a long wait," she said with a flirty giggle.

"When will he be back?"

"He got an emergency phone call from New York yesterday afternoon for a meeting there this morning. He said he might be back Friday."

I didn't know whether to get angry or laugh. So I laughed.

"Can he be reached by phone?"

"No sir, he is totally out of touch. The meeting in New York must really be important. He said he does not want to be bothered with anything. And boy was he firm with that."

"I hear you. He can be brusque at times."

"Nicely said," she replied. "Can I leave a message for him and let him know you were looking for him?"

"Thanks, but I was just in the area and wanted to surprise him. So there's no need to say a word. And thank you."

On my drive back to Sarasota across the Sunshine Skyway Bridge the weather was crystal clear and the traffic was clipping along the highway but I was in a deep fog. I called RH and told him the Aston Martin wasn't available for pick up last night. He understood. That was simple but why wasn't Louie there, so I could've gotten this over?

***

As I drove around the corner toward my house, my fog burned off quickly. Dijon and his flunky Gorman were across the street from the house, leaning on the Mercedes jawing about my property. My instinct was to leave the guy in pieces in the street but I knew that was not smart, so I controlled the urge. I pulled in the driveway, got out of the SUV and proceeded directly across the street toward Dijon. He made no move to leave.

I approached looking directly at Dijon's stony, pale face and into his shallow eyes.

"Well gentlemen, what brings you to a nice neighborhood like this? Anything I can help you with?"

Dijon's stance was rigid, trying not to flinch as his thin small, tight mouth opened to spew out his venom.

"We're just admiring the collateral for the mortgage I will hold in short order. You've done a professional renovation job. It would be a shame to lose such a property," Dijon said sarcastically.

Again, I did temper control and tried to feign civility.

"Listen Dijon, I think we got off on the wrong track maybe we can startover and work more amicably."

"And I'm sure that boy of yours would cry his eyes out if he couldn't sleep in that perfect room you built and decorated for him. Such a shame. Wouldn't that be a shame, Gorman?"

Gorman stood up like a puppet that just had its strings pulled. "Yes sir, a real shame. Poor boy."

I took a step closer to Dijon, not enough to clearly

threaten him but enough to physically state my rebuttal. He backed up and rested his hand on his car for support. I wanted to let him have it about stalking Camille and the tail he's had on us but I remained quiet. Silence was a better tactic.

After a tense silence, I asked him directly, "If you do actually close the deal with Frank Mangello, what arrangements could we make for me to catch up with the mortgage?"

"Let me make this perfectly clear," Dijon said with complete and vindictive arrogance. "My firm intention is to get you out of your little love bungalow as quickly as possible, tear it down to the ground and then build a suitable building for such a beautiful lot. So I advise you to start looking for a tent you can afford for you and your perfect boy and…your French paramour."

Okay, the gloves were off. "Your right about that shame part Napoleon." He twitched at the sound of his name. " I assure you, it wouldn't be pretty if something happened and we couldn't live here anymore. And you're right about another thing. My son's room is perfect for him. It seems your smarter than you look." I caught Gorman flinch out of the corner of my eye but Dijon remained physically stern but his eyes quivered. Then he recovered.

"Mr. Shaw. Your determination to keep this house ---"

"Shut up Napoleon Dijon, I've had enough of you!" It appeared as if I struck him across the face with a pair of dueling gloves. He growled a mumble to himself in French.

My hands flew out of my pockets but I held steady

and looked at him with vengeance. I stood still and took a few deep breaths. I knew I had to control myself. I didn't want to threaten him with Gorman standing there. I continued to stare hard right into his sour face. I wanted him to go to sleep in fear. I wanted his subconscious to be uneasy, restless and guarded in the night. He looked like he was afraid to move.

"Napoleon Bonaparte Dijon, I suggest you get your French haute-couture ass my off block. I've seen it get real dangerous around here, like a severe mistral wind blowing through Marseille. "

"Can we leave now?" Gorman meekly asked Dijon.

"I agree with Mr. Gorman it's time for you to leave."

They quickly got in the car and speed off. I wished Gorman wasn't present. I would have really enjoyed myself.

I got in the house and felt heat fill my body. My stomach tightened like steel. I needed badly to release my hate. I went into the garage, grabbed the dumbbells and pumped iron. After twenty minutes, I put the gloves on and began to beat on poor old Henry. I saw Dijon's face in the bag and punched it into oblivion. If it only could have actually been him… Maybe some day.

Ethan's bicycle stood against the wall. I remembered buying it years ago with only a few dollars left in my pocket. We got through that wormhole and we'll get through this one. I had promised Ethan we wouldn't lose our home. I promised him…

***

After dinner Ethan went in his room to finish his homework. I glanced at Camille across the table. Her face held guilt from chin to forehead.

"Jake, I'm sorry. I'm really sorry. All I can think of is that I'm the reason for what seems to be a vendetta against you from this psychopath Dijon. If I'd only ---"

"What Camille? What? Give into his demands? Don't do that to yourself. On my side, I opened an opportunity for him to strike. On your side, you did nothing. You just said, no. You did nothing that a normal man couldn't understand. Nothing of course, other than being irresistible."

The guilt dropped from her forehead but clung to her mouth where a small smile tried to make its way.

"Camille, you have touched me in places I've never been touched before. Baby, you have me for life. The more I learn about Dijon, the more I know that he has a bug up his tight ass, eating him raw, and it makes him a miserable son of bitch."

"And he's mean Jake. He's a mean man and I don't want you getting hurt."

"Here's the deal Ms. Camille Bissette. Somehow we've been given this jerk to deal with together and there's no way we're going to lose. I don't know how, but I sure believe Napoleon Dijon is going to meet his own Waterloo. And we're going to rise high above the Arc de Triumph. That's a promise."

Ethan must have over heard me promise and said, "And dad keep his promises. I know."

CHAPTER 28

"Odin, I've been doing exactly what you've suggested and nothing has changed. Nothing. I studied about the big bang and understand it. I meditated on the expression of Source within me. And I imagined and rehearsed that my desire was fulfilled but nothing. Nothing, nada, zip, zero."

Odin wasn't the slightest bit fazed by my rant. He didn't say a word to me. He just kept walking while watching a sizeable yacht coming into the marina.

"Did you hear what I said? Odin?"

Without missing a stride he turned and looked me straight in the eyes. "Yes Jake. I heard what you said."

"Well what gives?"

We walked about a hundred yards before he spoke. "You move like an athlete. Did you play a sport?"

"Baseball. I was a pitcher."

"Did you throw a curve ball?"

"Sure did. A damn good one."

"When you were shown how to throw it, were you

able to throw the curve with precision?"

"You have to be joking. It took a ton of practice for me to be able to get a handle on it."

"Jake, this spiritual process you are going through is light years more complicated that throwing a curve ball. It takes practice, repetition or as they say in the acting profession, many rehearsals. It's a cumulative process which takes time Jake, it takes time."

"How much time? I don't have a lot of time," I growled. "My life is on the verge of collapse. So how much time and for what? For the director to arrange things the way they need to be?"

Again he let me vent, he listened and didn't immediately respond. We walked in the weight of silence that would have sunk a ship. Then finally he answered me.

"No Jake, the director of your movie is the same director who created the universe. You're not waiting for Source to get his act together. Source is waiting for you to get your act together, to be the vessel of expression for your happy ending. And as far as how long that will take, sometimes it happens quickly, other times it takes longer and then sometimes it doesn't happen at all, simply because the actor is not up to playing his role well enough and he doesn't understand or believe in the 'unseen to seen,' law we talked about and hence didn't do his homework. He simply didn't rehearse enough, and,…and…and perhaps he didn't trust his director."

"So what you're saying is to trust my Higher Power and let go of the how and let go of the time factor, the when?" I asked impatiently.

"Yes. Jake realize deep in your bones, deep in your soul that you're dealing with the infinite intelligence of the universe. It's Source expressing through you, it works in ways you don't understand. When you let go of needing to know how it's going to get done, the universe conspires to help you by arranging the plot so people, places and things show up for your benefit. Things can happen in ways you could never have imagined and at the perfect time."

I took a deep breath and began to calm down. "I'll work on it."

"Good, because it's a huge understanding to grasp. Don't believe me. Test it. You do it and you'll know for yourself."

"Now what about my rehearsals. I'm trying hard---"

"Stop right there. There's no trying allowed. Trying is counter-productive."

"Then how…what do I do?"

"You use your imagination and pretend like I said. Daydream about your happy ending. Play make-believe like you did when you were a kid. Didn't you ever daydream about pitching a perfect game or hitting the winning home run?"

"I sure did and I actually pitched a perfect game in a sandlot league. And I did hit a few game winning home runs."

"That's what I'm talking about. When you're pretending, you're not trying, you're having fun. It feels good. Relax and get in an imaginative zone and daydream your ending. Again in acting parlance, rehearse and have fun with it."

"I know I can do that."

"Understand Jake, you have no power in this deal. Your job is to keep focused on what you want and not on what you don't want. The process works fluidly when you are relaxed. No trying, no forcing. Just be willing to receive your happy ending. Feel your happy ending and feel it true. True, like it already happened."

"Feel it true."

"Yes. Have you ever had something that you wanted come true? True has a tone, a feeling different than expectation. True feels solid, like it's a done deal. Feel that way about your happy ending and trust in your director. Jake, be Onederful."

"Got it."

***

Buoyed by Odin's inspiration, I headed to Tampa again to tell Louie I had changed my mind about entering the business. In my heart, I knew that getting back in that racket was not the best thing for me but then again there was the money, always the money, which I desperately needed. Even if it was a bit ethereal, to say the least, Odin had give me a process to get out of my mess and my trust in what Odin said was getting stronger.

On the Howard Franklin Bridge approaching Tampa my phone rang. It was Mangello.

"Hey Frank. How are you?"

"I'm better every minute but I don't think you'll be when I tell you what's happening?"

My trust started to sink into Tampa Bay.

"What's up Frank?"

"This morning I met with Dijon. He is more aggressive than ever to close this deal. He set a firm date. I'm sorry to tell but nineteen days from today he will own your mortgage."

Mangello's words punched me in my solar plexus, knocking the wind out of me.

"Jake? Jake? Are you there?"

"I'm here Frank. I'm here and I hear you. Gotta go now."

My trust was now sinking deeply, approaching the bottom of the bay. All the chips were on the table and the dice were in my hands. It was my roll. Trust? Who or what do I trust, Odin's tutor-ledge of a metaphysical law or the sure green cash of Villani Enterprises? I was three-quarters over the bridge heading toward Tampa with no way of turning around.

***

Fifteen minutes later I pulled into the parking lot of Villani Enterprises. Do I turn the car around and head to back to Sarasota or…?

When I walked into the lobby, I immediately saw the look on Ms. Roma's face but before she could speak, I did.

"I know. I know. Mr Villani doesn't like surprises but he's got one and he'll just have to deal with it."

"But---"

"No buts. Please just tell him I'm here."

"But---"

This time she was interrupted by the presence of the

grizzled, Louis Villani himself, coming through the front door. When he saw me, a hard looked crossed his face. He pointed to me and snarled, "I want to talk with you. Follow me."

I followed him into a small, unused office on the first floor. He pointed to an empty chair and I sat.

"There's been a change," he said in coarse voice. The organization is changing quickly."

"What happened?"

"The business here in Tampa is going to be handled by Joe Bell. I gotta go to New York for awhile." He slowly shook his head and snarled, "There's no room for you here. Forget about this place."

"What happened Louie?"

My question didn't land. "I have things to do," he said as he walked toward the door.

"That's it? Nothing else?" I asked.

His sneer was loud enough for me to hear and I knew better than to challenge it. It was over, that quickly. He turned and walked away leaving me sitting in the chair.

***

Driving back to Sarasota thoughts raced through my head, I never expected something like that to happen. I wondered about Odin's words about how the plot would be arranged for my happy ending. I couldn't help but think that maybe, just maybe, there was something really going on behind the scenes.

CHAPTER 29

"Dad, dad what time is practice?"

"Eleven and Blackie's coming to watch you."

"Cool. He'll see how much better I am now."

"He sure will, son."

"What time is it now?"

"Almost ten, so you've got thirty minutes to get your gear together and get dressed."

"Gotcha, I'll be ready."

My phone rang and the ID glowed private number. I let it ring twice, then picked it up.

"Jake Shaw."

"Jake Shaw from Munroe Realty?"

"That's me."

"My name is Miriam Nemeth."

"How can I help you?"

"You can meet me today at noon at the Palm Restaurant on St. Armand's Circle?"

"Excuse me?"

"I would like you to meet me at the Palm Restaurant

at noon today. Mr. Verzi recommended I meet you. Time is of the essence."

"Do you mean Bill Verzi?"

"Yes, Mr. Bill Verzi."

I hadn't talked with Bill Verzi in years but my respect for him was immense, if he wanted her to meet with me, count me in.

"Yes, I'll be there. Your name again, please?

"Miriam Nemeth."

"How will I recognize you?"

"Long silver hair and I'll be wearing a red blouse. And I know what you look like Mr. Shaw. Good bye."

I grabbed my decaf and sat on a kitchen stool. Bill Verzi, I didn't even know if he was still alive. I had a sense this was going to be interesting.

Then there was a knock at the kitchen door. Before I could move, the door opened and Blackie bounced into the kitchen.

"Thought I'd get here early. Hope you don't mind, but even if you do, I'm already here. Got some coffee left?"

"Decaf."

"It'll do."

I got his Yankees cup and filled it up.

"You look a little puzzled buddy boy, what's going on?"

"I just got a strange call from a woman, who wants to meet me at the Palm at noon today."

"Camille's a friend of mine. Don't you go screwing up a good thing Jake boy."

I almost spit the coffee out of my mouth, choking on his remark.

"Get your mind out of 42nd Street. This is business."

"How do you know? What gives you a clue detective?"

"She mentioned a man from my past who I had business dealings with, and from then, we developed a friendship. Even though she didn't say what she wanted, that was enough for me to meet with her. Now I need to you to watch Ethan while I meet with her. Can you handle it?"

"Under one condition."

"What's that?"

"Well you know, I really don't like the kid and he don't like me."

"That's obvious. What's the condition?"

"That after his practice, I can take him to lunch with me down on the beach."

"Damn, Blackie you're a martyr, a veritable saint."

"Yeah, I know. What can I say?"

***

At 11: 55 a.m. the Palm Restaurant was already packed with tourists looking to fill their bellies before doing more shopping on St. Armand's Circle. I spotted Miriam Nemeth immediately. Her elegance stood out.

"Hello Mr. Shaw. I'm Miriam Nemeth." She offered me her bejeweled hand. I took it.

"Please call me Jake, Ms. Nemeth."

"Miriam. Not Ms. Nemeth."

I was anxious to know what this is about but didn't want to appear too blunt.

"Miriam, it's been awhile since I talked with Mr. Verzi, how is he doing?"

"He's doing well. He's in Venice painting."

"He's in Venice? Just down the road?

"Not Venice, Florida. Venice, Italy. He turned 90 this year and wanted to spend this part of his life enjoying his roots. So he moved to Venice two years ago."

"The beauty of Venice must make him very happy. He's a good man."

I took a sip of water, put the glass down and had to get to the point.

"Ms. Nemeth, I mean Miriam, I don't want to be blunt but why am I here?"

She grinned. "Mr. Verzi told me you don't beat around the bush. He also told me that you were also an honorable, noble man. A man of integrity and that I must meet you."

This time she took a sip of water. She looked like she could be on the cover of Elle.

"Mr. Verzi told me you have a son. How old is he?"

"Ethan is ten."

"Mr. Verzi also told you me you were a single father."

"A single father not by choice. Ethan's mother died."

"I'm sorry to hear that."

"Thank you, but again I'm asking, why am I here? Why are we talking?"

She gazed off, appearing absent, not hearing my question.

"Miriam?"

"I'm sorry Jake, I was thinking of my daughter. She

was ten when she died in a car accident. I was a single parent too for about eight years. I understand how difficult it can be."

"Now I'm sorry to hear about your loss. I don't know how I'd react if that happened to me."

"After the accident, to deal with the sorrow I put all my energy into business, something I understand and do well. My father was a very prominent and successful man and he taught me the ways of the world including how to read financial statements and negotiate deals. And… that's why you're here Jake. I'm interested in Sarasota. I like it. Even though we are in the middle of a terrible economic crisis, I know something value when I see it. Mr. Verzi also told me you know real estate."

"I know some, yes."

"Do you mind if I ask you some questions?"

"That's fine."

For the next thirty minutes, as we ate, she grilled me on my real estate knowledge in general and specifically the Sarasota market. She covered commercial real estate, raw land, land development, condominiums, shopping centers, office buildings, financing. She asked me hypothetical questions on multiple scenarios. It was more intense than taking the Florida brokers exam. When she concluded with my oral examination, she stood up and excused herself. "I need to go to the ladies room."

I had no idea what grade she gave me, but I gave her the straightest answers I could. If I didn't know, I told her that too. One thing I did know for certain, I was ready to conclude our meeting.

When she came back from the rest room, she was a different woman. It was if she dropped her briefcase and picked up a designer handbag. "Jake, would you like some dessert?"

"No thank you. I'm good and I really must be going. I have to pick up Ethan."

"Jake I want to thank you for coming today. Mr. Verzi is a fine judge of character. I'm glad we met." She extended her hand and I shook it.

"I thank you as well. I hope this was a beneficial meeting for you," I said.

"It most certainly was. Thank you. Good bye."

***

When I got back to the house, I was surprised to see Blackie and Ethan there.

"I thought you two dudes would be at lunch on the beach."

"That's the plan, however, that son of yours got so dirty scooping up ground balls, he needed a quick shower. So ya want to join us?"

"I just finished eating with that woman, no food for me, but I could use a cold beer."

Blackie agreed. "A cold beer sounds good to me. And you can tell me about your meeting with the strange lady. What'd she want?"

"I'm not sure. She might be kicking tires."

"A tire kicker eh?"

"A very elegant tire kicker."

"You never can tell buddy boy. You never know."

CHAPTER 30

It was Monday morning, I was making Ethan's breakfast, when the phone rang. It was a private caller.

"Jake Shaw."

"Jake, this is Miriam Nemeth. Come to my suite at the Ritz Carlton at noon."

"Noon?"

"And Jake..."

"Yes."

"Clear the rest of the afternoon. You'll be busy."

It sounded like an order.

"Doing what?"

"You'll understand. See you at noon," she said and hung up.

Through the years I learned to pick out the tire kickers early before I'd waste too much time. However, I wasn't getting a clear read on Miriam Nemeth. I had to trust Bill Verzi.

I heard Ethan banging around in his room.

"Ethan, how you doing in there buddy. You don't

want to be late for school."

"Aw dad, yes I do. How about I get there at 3 today?"

"You are one funny little man."

"I know that. I'm deciding whether I want to be a comic or a baseball player."

"My advice to you is not to throw your baseball glove away."

"Now you're funny. Is my breakfast almost ready? I'm starved."

"Come and get it little buddy."

***

At noon I approached the desk at the Ritz Carlton. After a quick security call to Ms. Nemeth, I was escorted to her suite.

"Jake, come in." She pointed to a couch. "Over there."

It was a long leather couch. I sat at one end, she sat at the opposite end.

"Jake, like yourself, I believe in getting to the point quickly. I enjoyed meeting you Saturday. Mr. Verzi told me good things about you but I wanted to sample the goods myself. Since I was a little girl, I watched my father size up people and size up deals. He had an uncanny ability to walk away when needed or to plunge in and get started. I not only learned from him, I also inherited his abilities. I'm confident that I'm correct in my appraisal of you. So I want you to handle something for me."

"And what may that be?"

"This real estate market is terrible and I aim to take advantage of it."

"How so?"

"One of things I learned from my father was to be a contrarian and go against the market. He made a fortune doing so and I've followed in his footsteps."

She reached into a briefcase and pulled out some papers.

"Here is a contract for a piece of land I want to buy near Lakewood Ranch. Have a look. Here also is the selling sheet."

I took them both from her hand. I scanned the selling sheet. The asking price for the WBA Ranch was $14,000,000. My breath stopped but I mindfully held a stoic expression on my face. Then I perused the contract. Munich Investments Inc. offered $8,750,000 for the purchase of WBA Ranch. The rest of the contract was clean, without contingencies and with a closing scheduled within two weeks. I couldn't find a financing strategy. At the bottom it showed Munroe Realty as the buying broker with a 5% commission. I lost my breath again but regained it quickly because I was sure this contract wouldn't fly. I put the contract down on the coffee table.

"What do you think about the contract Jake?"

I searched for words of diplomacy. "I do have concerns."

"They are?"

"It's pretty straight forward that's for sure, but...but the offer is far below the asking price. So far below that reasonable negotiations may never take place."

"Anything else?"

"A second concern is financing. I see no strategy for financing and the chance of a bank financing raw land in this economic climate is…well…next to none."

I scratched my head, took a deep breath and kept my bearing.

"Jake I know that this is not what you're used to but it's the way I do business. And successfully I might add. So as I have decided to trust you, you need to decide to trust me. As for a financing strategy, there is none. It's a cash deal."

I picked the contract back up.

"Two questions. What is Munich Investments Inc.? And, the contract is signed by Ruth Schultz, who is she?"

"Munich Investments is the holding company started by my father, of which, I am the sole shareholder. And I am Ruth Schultz. That is my legal, birth given name. Miriam is my middle name Nemeth is my divorced husband's name, which I took when I married but gave up when my daughter died. I still use it for various purposes, including keeping my business ventures private. And that is to be held in private by you. Understood?"

"Understood."

"I'm sure your mind is reeling with more questions, which I will answer when you return with the signed contract. But for now you know all you need to know to get the contract signed by the seller. Here is an escrow check for $250,000. That should suffice for a two week closing. Now you have work to do Jake Bring me back a signed contract."

"Miriam?"

"Yes."

"I'm going to be blunt. The chances of this contract being accepted are less than none."

"But, you will present my offer."
"That I will do."

***

When I got to my car, I sat for awhile. Was this woman for real? The contract was over $5,000,000 less than the asking price. There was no way in hell that I was going to get this signed but I did have a fiduciary responsibility to present the contract to the seller, even if I got thrown out of the broker's office This deal was so ridiculous to me, I didn't even want to calculate the commission but I did. It was $437,500. I calculated it again. Same number. I'd get 90% of that, $393,750, almost $400,000! This had to be a joke of some kind.

I called the listing broker, Joe Shapiro, and told him I was coming in with a contract. He sounded like an arrogant bastard. When I arrived at his office, my sense was confirmed.

***

"There's no way I'm presenting this piece of shit offer to my seller. This isn't even worth the time of a phone call," Shapiro said.

I expected nothing less but I reminded him, "I understand your sentiment but we do have to present any and all offers, even if they seem insulting. So make the phone call, so we can put this to rest."

He looked at me with anger in his eyes, knowing I was right. He threw the contract down on his desk, picked up the phone and called his seller.

"Hello Mr. Axelrod… Listen I'm holding an offer here for the ranch. It's a shit offer, and I apologize for presenting it to you, but by real estate law I have to present all offers. But in professional opinion there's no way you can accept this crap."

It seemed Shapiro was arrogant with everyone.

"Yes sir Mr. Axelrod. The offer is for $8,750,000. That's $5,250,000 below the asking price…Yes sir I know you can do the math." Shapiro then listened. "I don't know. After I saw the price I stopped reading, let me see…there doesn't seem to be any contingencies but I don't see any terms or financing strategies."

I interjected, "It's a cash deal. No financing. Cash. Two weeks closing. Take it or leave it."

"Please hold on Mr. Axelrod the buyer's agent is here and he's talking to me." Shapiro cupped the phone in his hand and looked at me. "What did you say?"

"Cash deal. No financing. No negotiating. Close in two weeks," I repeated.

Shapiro squinted his eyes like I was crazy.

"Mr. Axelrod, he says it's a cash deal, take it or leave it. Closing in two weeks…Yes sir, cash…two weeks… Yes sir."

When Shapiro hung up, he shook his head in confusion. "He wants me to bring him the contract right now. And I want you to come with me just in case I need you or if he wants to see the lunatic who brought me this contract."

We got into Shapiro's Mercedes and headed to Axelrod's home. The fifteen minute drive to Lido Key was all I could handle listening to Shapiro. I kept reminding myself to be patient for the $393,750 possibility. I'd deal with Shapiro for a short while, in exchange for being done with Napoleon Bonaparte Dijon forever.

When we arrived at Axelrod's gulf front mansion on West Way Drive, Shapiro told me to stay in the car. If he needed me, I'd be summoned. Other than his attitude, that worked for me. After ten minutes of waiting, I decided to walk along the street of the luxurious homes banked up against the Gulf of Mexico. The street was certainly top of the line Sarasota. As I walked, Odin came to mind along with the many words he shared with me, which seemed incongruous with the world on West Way Drive. But on the other hand maybe it wasn't incongruous at all.

I walked about a mile and then headed back to the car. On the way back I saw Shapiro driving toward me. He had a stunned look on his face.

"What happened with Axelrod?" I asked.

"He signed the damn contract." He was shaking his head. "He signed the damn contract. I can't fucking believe it."

I got in the car and sat in disbelief along with Shapiro. I too was stunned.

Shapiro continued, "He sat there and went through the contract. He said it was the cleanest contract he's ever seen. He took out his gold pen and signed all the copies and handed them to me and told me to get the ball rolling. I asked him why he had accepted such a low offer. He looked out toward the gulf and said, 'Fast nickels are better than slow dimes' and he took out a cigar and began to smile. It sure the hell surprised me."

By the time we got back to Shapiro's office, I was stoic. Even though I mentally understood what was happening, it didn't register emotionally with me. Maybe it was too big emotionally to grab hold of and with all my earlier deals tanking, I just couldn't allow my self to trust it.

**

Miriam Nemeth opened her door but didn't say a word. I handed her the signed contract also without saying a word. She turned quickly to the back page and saw the seller's signature. I expected a look of excitement or surprise on her face but she seemed to know that he'd sign it.

"You knew he'd sign it, didn't you?"

"Yes."

"How? How could you possibly expect him to sign it? And without even attempting to negotiate the price."

"I do my homework Jake. I do lots of homework. I research the property, I consult the planning department, I learn the pace of the market, analyze the present economic climate and gauge where it's heading. I also investigate the seller and this seller I investigated extensively. In his case, he's involved in various business ventures besides this ranch. In the midst of this economic straight jacket, he is over leveraged, under collateralized and severely strapped for cash. He has a number of loans coming due, some interest only, some with the entire principle due. Raw land doesn't produce income and that's part of the deal. He needs cash to pay the debts or else other investments would come tumbling down like dominoes. He's in imminent need of about seven million dollars. My offer, although vastly under both the asking price and the market value, will save the other interests he owns. He knows the relative value of cash. In his time of need, this is a good deal for him. He knows it, so he signed the contract."

I was blown away by her precision.

"But why me? What did you need me for? My commission is substantial, why not just go through the listing office and take it off the table?"

"For three reasons. First, I do not like nor do I trust the listing broker. And I do not do business with people I don't like or trust. Included in this deal, as you stated, is a sizeable commission and I simply don't want them to have it. Secondly, I am a private person and I only work with people who value discretion. Mr. Verzi said you can be highly discreet and so far you have proven him correct. Third, I see long term potential in the Sarasota area and I want to develop a long term working arrangement with someone who is professional, highly competent and whom I can trust. Again, at Mr. Verzi's suggestion, hopefully that will be you. The commission you will receive for this deal, although way out of proportion for the work you did for it, will serve as evidence of my willingness to reward such a person. Any other questions?"

"Yes, what are you going to do with the property?"

She glanced at her watch. "That's a conversation we will have at a later date. First let's get this deal closed. My private attorney will contact you. You'll like working with him."

"Private attorney?"

"Yes, he works directly with and only for me." Again she looked at her watch. "Your boy is waiting for you. I suggest you go home."

I shook my head in amazement. "I don't know what to say to you other than…thank you."

She just nodded her head. "Go home to your boy."

When I got in my car I took a deep breath and began to laugh. I took out my calculator and hit the numbers again. "$393, 750."

***

That evening after I got Ethan to bed, I called Frank Mangello.

"Hi Frank. How are you doing?"

"I've been sweating my ass off until this deal gets closed with Dijon. And I know, I know that's not what you want to hear but I need it badly."

"Yes, I know. So what's going on?"

"Well Jake, the deal is set to close on Monday in two weeks."

"Hold on Frank, I just put together a deal, a big deal. A deal that'll make us both flush. And it's going to close quickly."

"How quick?"

"Hopefully in less than two weeks. I know it sounds crazy but it came out of the blue."

"Deals that come out of the blue usually are crazy. Jake, I'm glad for you but unless I get money in my hand before I close with Dijon, he'll hold your mortgage. I wish the best for you but you and I both know the state of the economy and I've got to go with the money. Keep me posted Jake. If anything good happens let me know. And I'll keep you abreast of any changes on my end. Good night Jake."

I put the phone down and headed to the kitchen for a drink. I had the thought that Mangello was right. What if it didn't close? It was kind of unbelievable. Who'd believe it? What if Miriam didn't have the millions in cash to close the deal? It did seem too screwy to be true.

But then I had another thought. Wasn't this exactly what Odin meant by the arrangement of the plot? Could Odin be right?

CHAPTER 31

Blackie didn't see me come in. He was too busy flirting with the cute waitress wearing the tight Moe's Place t-shirt. As I approached Blackie's table, she spotted me, blushed and retreated to the kitchen.

"You sure have a way with women Mr. Blackburn."

"I sure enjoy playing with them but I sure don't want to keep any of them. My relationship skill level is like a first grader trying to read Latin."

"Close, but maybe not that bad."

"You got your running shoes on, you've been out running this morning?"

"No. I went over to the park to see if I could find Odin."

"You mean the voodoo man."

"I wanted to tell him the goods news but he wasn't there. In fact he hasn't been there for a week or so."

"Good news? Tell me man, tell me."

The waitress came back over to the table with a twinkle in her eye and heated up Blackie's coffee and brought me a decaf.

"So Jake my boy, give, give the news."

"I've been practicing some of Odin's suggestions and ---"

He interrupted me, "Odin-shmodin."

I continued unfazed. "And get this. A little over a week ago, I get a phone call from a woman, who was referred to me by an old friend of mine. To bottom line it, in a matter of two days I have a signed contract for almost nine million dollars on a chunk of land east of the highway."

"You gotta be kidding?"

"I'm as serious as a bank overdraft."

Blackie slams the table shaking the cups. "Damn! Damn! Damn!.... That's terrific! Way to go!" Then he sits straight up. " But, but... wait a second. How's she going to get financing in this market for raw land?"

"She's not. Get this. She's paying cash."

"You're bull shitting me."

"No sir, I'm not."

"She's going to ante up the cash at the closing table?"

"How long you have to wait until that happens? Two years?"

"Two days."

"I don't believe a word of it."

"The proof will be two days from today. In the afternoon, Thursday."

Blackie sat back in his chair, stretched out and rubbed his head.

"You ain't kidding me, are you?"

"Not in the slightest."

My cell phone rang. It was Mangello.

"Hey Frank what's up?"

"Jake, I just want to remind you that I'm closing with Dijon next Monday at 3 PM. How's your dealing coming?"

"We're on schedule to close this Thursday. So cross your fingers it gets done."

"I'm happy for your Jake but I have to tell you again, if you don't close, I'm going through with Dijon on Monday. I can't wait any longer."

"I hear you Frank. No worries. Good-bye."

Blackie saw my worried face, didn't match my good news.

"What are you worried about Jake? If this a good deal, you have a closing Thursday, pay Mangello and kiss off Dijon."

"Blackie, the reality is that right now real estate closing tables aren't the most stable of platforms. And, being honest with myself, I've had so many deals hit the bricks in the past couple of years, that until the cash in my hands, I'm skeptical. And that's not saying anything about the size or weirdness of this deal. So if something goes wrong and Mangello closes with Dijon, my life is going to be a damn nightmare."

"No kidding. That French stench is a sociopath. If that dude was coming at me, I'd prepare for the worst and when I could, I'd let him have it right between the eyes."

"That really gives me confidence."

"Oh, sorry about that," he laughed.

"Let's change the subject. How's Bobby doing? Have you talked to him lately?"

"Yea, I talked with him last night. He's doing good. He's really into the Yankees like his pop. It was so great hanging with him, even if it was on the phone. But when we finished, I got depressed. I drank a six-pack and watched the movie the Terminator for about the tenth time."

"Too bad the Terminator isn't a friend of mine. I'd let him handle Dijon." I relaxed back on the chair and laughed. "Wouldn't that be great?"

Blackie imitated my posture and smiled. "No worries Jake. No worries."

CHAPTER 32

The secretary led me down a long corridor toward the conference room of the offices of Street and Fenner, Attorneys at Law. I heard people arguing inside the conference room but when the door opened, silence seized the room. Before me sat Joe Shapiro and another man.

"It's about time you got here Shaw. We've been here fifteen minutes. Where's your attorney with the money or do you have it?" Shapiro was his acerbic self.

I ignored Shapiro and focused on the other man. I extended my hand. "I'm Jake Shaw."

"I'm Bill Axelrod. Nice to meet you Mr. Shaw."

Michael Street, attorney at law and president of the title company closing the deal entered the room. We introduced ourselves.

"Gentlemen, we need to wait until Marshall Deacon arrives, with the documents and a check from the buyer," Street said. "And we're also waiting for another delivery before we can begin. So until then… I see you all have coffee except for you Mr. Shaw. Would you like a coffee?"

"Decaf please."

"I'll have some brought right in. I'll be back just as soon as the last minute details get wrapped up."

As each minute went by I saw the blood vessels in Shapiro's face get thicker and darker but Bill Axelrod remained calm without the slightest sign of concern. I practiced my stoic face, as my stomach did a whirling dervish dance.

Fifteen minutes later, Michael Street re-entered the room.

"Gentlemen we have a two situations here. The first is obvious without Mr. Deacon's representation and a check, we have no buyer present."

"Damn it Shaw, I knew you didn't know what you were doing," blustered Shapiro.

Again I ignored the yapping dog behind the fence. I asked Street, "And what is the second situation?"

"We've been waiting for Federal Express to arrive with a pertinent document. They just left here but did not have the document and from what the driver said, that was his last trip to this office for today."

"And what's the document?" Axelrod asked.

"Bill, your brother Malcolm failed to return the release needed for the transfer of title. I spoke with him Monday and after a bit of a hemming and hawing, he assured me that he would get them here in time."

Axelrod didn't flinch but his eyes hardened. Before he could speak Shapiro blurted out to Axelrod, "I told you he would be trouble. I told you."

Axelrod focused his attention at Shapiro and in a

calm, rational tone said, "That's enough."

Shapiro slumped like a scolded dog. Axelrod turned to me and calmly asked, "Do you have any idea what's going on your end Mr. Shaw?"

"Honestly, Mr. Axelrod I do not. Yesterday everything was ready to go. Please let me call Mr. Deacon."

"Please do."

Before I could hit the call button, Deacon called me. "Jake Shaw."

"Jake, Marshall Deacon here. I am terribly sorry I'm late. For the purposes of time, I'll explain when I get there which should be in twenty minutes."

"Marshall, there's no need to bother today. For other reasons we need to re-schedule. I'll tell you why later. I'll call you when we're done here."

I looked at both Axelrod and Street. "Mr. Deacon apologizes. He was detained for reasons not relevant now but he was planning to be here in twenty minutes.

"I see," Axelrod said. "So the deal is still good?"

"Yes sir," I confirmed.

"Then the ball is my court. Mr. Shaw please be assured, I'm not like my brother. If I say I'm going to do something, I will most certainly do it. Understand I cannot guarantee you that I can I get my brother's signature on the needed documents but I will guarantee you that I will make his life a living hell if he doesn't sign exactly what he needs to sign. And he will feel the heat as soon as I leave this room." He offered his hand to me.

I shook it and added. "That's good enough for me."

"Then it seems we have a live deal again." Michael

Street said. "I will get it to the closing table as soon as I get the release from Malcolm.

I took a deep breath. Although I wasn't walking out with a check, I wasn't dead in the water. We all left the room in silence, especially Shapiro who seemed muzzled, at least for the moment.

Driving home I called Mangello.

"Hey Frank, I need a big favor…"

"I'm assuming this call is to tell me your big deal fell through. Listen Jake, I told you I can't give you any more time. It's impossible. I'm sorry I really am but there's no way in hell I'm not closing Monday at 3. Do you understand?

"I hear you loud and clear. Loud and clear. I'll talk to you later Frank."

That morning I had felt so much hope for the day. After the delay, I still had a little hope but now I had no idea when this deal would close or if for certain it would. I was emotionally drained, bone tired and I felt like a fool for giving hope to the situation.

***

When I pulled into the driveway, I saw a big congratulations banner strung across the portico. I took a deep breath and let out a sigh. Nothing like being the guy who strikes out in the bottom of the ninth with two outs and bases loaded. The front door opened before I got to it, with Camille, Blackie and Ethan standing in front me applauding. The applause stopped when they saw my face.

"Sorry guys, there's no need to applaud. The job

didn't get done."

"Why? What happened darling? You dear man."

I explained as quickly as I could, including my conversation with Mangello. I needed a little escape so I headed to the kitchen and poured myself a bourbon.

Blackie followed me in. "Pour me one of those too."

I poured a shot for him and a double for me.

He belted his down and handed me the glass to fill it.

"Jake, the ball game ain't over till it's over. There's still a few innings left. Something will happen, you'll see."

"Thanks for your optimism. "

Camille entered the kitchen and said, "Now is when miracles happen."

"And I'm expecting one," I said with a thumbs up sign.

"Just like Camille said, that's when they happen." Blackie confirmed.

"Where did Ethan go?" I asked.

"In his room," Camille said.

I went into Ethan's room to check on him. He was sprawled out on the bed with a sullen look on his face.

"Listen little buddy, I don't know how this is going to work out but I do know that in time things will be the best ever. You just have to keep believing."

"Even when you're losing by a lot of runs?" he asked.

"Even then. Especially then."

"Ok dad, if you say so. I believe you."

"I say so slugger. I say so."

The truth was I needed to believe that more myself. So I sat with him for few minutes, took a few deep breaths, held him in my arms and rehearsed my happy ending.

CHAPTER 33

Saturday morning I sat on the bench at the entrance of the park waiting for Odin. I needed clarity. I needed to understand why I got so close to my happing ending and presto it was gone, which was certainly not a happy ending.

After five minutes of waiting, Odin entered the park. We exchanged greetings and walked while I explained to him what happened at the closing. I also told him of my confusion and dismay. As always, he listened intently until I finished talking, before he spoke.

"Questions for you Jake."

"Shoot."

"You understand that your life is like a movie, right?

"Yes, and right now not a happy one.

"When you were pretending, rehearsing, did you have doubts that your happing ending would take place?"

"After all the deals that tanked on me in the past couple of years, sure I had doubts. Truthfully, it would have surprised me if the deal did close. As terrible as it sounds, I've gotten accustomed to things not working out."

"Jake, doubt is a vile pattern you can lock your self into. Doubt is a negative feeling, a vibration that draws to you exactly the opposite of what you want. Doubt is an unconscious watering of weeds. Years ago, it became clear to me that, 'If I live in doubt, I will do without.' "

"I can really live in doubt, big time," I confessed.

"Yes I understand. It absolutely takes a vigilant practice of rehearsing before that negative habit breaks.

When you want fulfillment but dwell in the consciousness of doubt, you have a lack of trust, which will indeed inhibit your fulfillment. That's the metaphysical law. The feeling of doubt is powerful and can override any mental desire you hold. It can cancel your happing ending. That's because what you feel is real and what you feel you will experience. To re-iterate, what you feel is real and because it's real, you will draw that experience to you."

We walked about a hundred yards in silence when a flock of parakeets flew over our heads and nested in a big oak tree.

"Those birds are beautiful aren't they? And, every once in awhile they bless us with their presence."

My thoughts were not on the birds but on the closing table and walking away with a fat check, paying Mangello, getting rid of Dijon and living happily ever after.

"Odin, what about the other people at that closing table, what's their part in the deal not closing? I didn't have anything to do with Axelrod's brother not sending in that release. Don't they have any responsibility in this situation?"

" Good question. Jake, it's your movie, not theirs. You are the writer and star of your movie. They are simply character actors playing supporting roles. You don't know their movie and you have no need to know. You don't need to know or understand how or why your director is arranging the plot in this way. Just trust and give it time to unfold.

Focus only on your movie. Focus on what you're feeling and your happy ending. Embody your happy ending, dance with it, make love with it, wallow in it, swim in it, feel it in your bones, feel it in your soul. Jake, make your vision palpable and feel joyous that it has happened."

"Like practicing a pick off move to first base."

"Yes. Do it mentally and emotionally like you're in a real game. Do so because your fulfillment has already taken place in the unseen, spiritual world and with consistent pretending, it will solidify into the seen, physical world. How it takes place is not your job. It's the job of your director. Let the mystery unfold."

"Slowly, I'm beginning to understand this process."

"Jake I'm going to say this again, this is all about waking up to the true expression of Source's energy within you and taking dominion over your own life. Wake up to your intimate union with the benevolent, infinitely intelligent, creative, malleable Substance of all, pulsating through you. It's about you being Onederful. Remember, Source is wanting and needing to express in the world through the fulfillment of your desires."

We walked to the end of the loop in silence. I was locked into the energy and possibility of Odin's words and thinking of my part and my responsibility in my movie. It sure presented a different perspective to live by.

As we approached the end Odin said, "One more time... feel your happy ending, feel it as if it has already happened and then feel immense gratitude for it".

"Sort of like the check is in the mail scenario."

"Positive expectation is one way to begin feeling, then move to feeling the check already in your hands. The feelings of each are different. Feel the difference in your breath as you do each. Experience it for yourself."

"Damn Odin, I think I'm actually starting to get what you've been saying all this time."

"That's a good thing Jake. As you do your homework and practice what we've talked about, you'll be able to understand more and begin to own it as yours. And in doing so, you'll see the proof really is in the pudding.

One last thing, in every area of your life, always being mindful of being Onederful, be aware of Spirit within you. The repeated affirmation, 'I am Onederful,' can be helpful in reminding you that you are indeed an expression of Source."

"Thank you. Thank you. Thank you."

***

It was about 2 pm when I returned from Ethan's game, I popped open a cold beer and said to Camille. "Something's not right. I can feel it."

"I assume you called him," she said.

It's not like him to miss Ethan's game."

"Did you call him?"

"Blackie never misses any of Ethan's games. He enjoys them too much, plus he gets his jollies yelling at the umpires."

"Jake, for the third time did you call him?"

"Yes babe, three times. I even drove by his condo on the way home but didn't see his truck."

Camille took the can of beer out of my hand and took a swig.

"Jake, you know better than I do, that Blackie can be unpredictable."

"But not about missing Ethan's games. Something's not right."

"Maybe he met a beautiful woman last night and he put out the do not disturb sign."

"Camille Bissette you are a dreamer, a romantic."

"I am indeed, a huge romantic. I'm still waiting for my knight in shining armor to ride up on his white horse and rescue me from the dragon," she said dramatically.

"Can he drive up in a white Toyota Highlander instead?" I asked, looking for a laugh but her face became sullen.

"Hey babe, why the quick change of mood?"

"Nothing. I'm alright. Where's Ethan?"

"You don't seem alright. What's up? Talk to me."

She sat down on a kitchen chair.

"It's just that…"

"Just what?"

She glanced at the kitchen clock on wall.

"In almost exactly forty eight hours Mangello will be closing his deal with Dijon and despite what you say, I still feel so responsible for bringing him into your life and ruining it."

Tears welled up in her eyes and she turned her back to me. I stepped forward and wrapped my arms around her.

"Camille my love, you are such a dear soul. And the truth is, if the economy didn't essentially collapse and Mangello didn't need the money, Dijon wouldn't be in my life and if I had the money to pay off Mangello, I'd be home free and clear. But I don't, it's that simple. Dijon senses a vulture deal with Mangello and he's swooping down to get it."

She faced me with tears running down her cheeks.

"But Dijon is the worst kind of ugly vulture and I don't want him in your life. He's horrible," she cried.

"Listen, last night I was watching the baseball game. The Rays were losing by four runs in the bottom of the ninth. They were batting with two out and two strikes. One more strike and they lose the game. Well, after fouling a ball into the left field stands, the batter hit a double to left center and then….and then….all with two outs… the Rays scored four runs to tie the game up. It was amazing. Talk about a great comeback."

I wiped the tears from her cheeks and kissed her gently on her lips. "And we can have a great comeback too." Her eyes stared to twinkle.

"Did they win the game?"

I backed away a bit and started to laugh.

"What? What? What's so funny? Did they win?"

I was still laughing, "No they lost in the tenth inning by four more runs."

She smacked me on the shoulder and laughed too. We both laughed so loud, releasing our stress. Ethan must have heard us laughing and ran into the kitchen.

"What's so funny? I haven't heard you guys laugh like that in a long time." And he joined in the laughter. "Tell me. What gives?"

We didn't say anything but continued to laugh until it hurt.

A few minutes later Camille said, "Ethan I have to run to the mall to pick up some art supplies, would you like to go with me?"

"If I can I get ice cream."

"Is that a bribe?"

"Yeah, sort of. Did it work?"

Camille laughed, "No."

"I just thought I'd try."

"Good try. What flavor are you going to get?"

"Camille. You're just like my dad. You're the best!"

***

With Camille and Ethan off to the mall, I decided to rehearse. I sprawled out on my bed and relaxed my body and relaxed my mind. I got in touch with my breath as I tracked my inhalation and then my exhalation. After a few minutes my whole being quieted down, the world of my senses faded and the door to my imagination slowly opened. I felt peaceful, calm and powerful; totally in control of my inner world, the source of my creativity. I imaginatively created and rehearsed the world I wanted, my future reality, my happy ending. And, it felt damn good.

CHAPTER 34

D-day arrived. Dijon day. Sure it wasn't the horror of the Normandy invasion, but to me it felt personally violent. I had done everything I possibly could to avoid Dijon from owning my mortgage. I sat in my kitchen and remembered it took me two months to renovate it with my own hands. To think that Dijon might come in and level our home, made my skin itch. Life tasted as horrid as the coffee I was drinking but I wasn't giving up. I had to stay positive, even if I felt like I was lying to myself. I closed my eyes and took a deep breath and nurtured the feeling that somehow, someway this had all worked out. Years ago, there was a major league pitcher who as his team advanced through the playoffs kept saying to anyone who'd listen, "Ya gotta believe. Ya gotta believe." As it turned out, he was the winning pitcher in the game his team won the World Series. So, I had to believe, even against all odds.

My plan was to pick Ethan up from school and take

him to the beach and tell him the situation. Unless my miracle happened before 3 pm, the axe was scheduled to fall and Dijon would be holding it. Vigilantly, I kept imagining my happy ending.

***

At 2:15, I picked up Ethan from school.

"Hey slugger, how'd you like to go to the beach?"

"You're kidding right?"

"Nope, I'm not kidding. Just you and me walking and hanging out at the beach. Maybe we can grab something to eat. What do you say?"

"Hmmm. I have lots of homework and I need to study. Hmmmm, okay if I must to go to the beach, I'll surrender and go," he said trying to stifle a laugh.

"What a surprise! Let's go."

We drove about five minutes and Ethan asked, "What's the holiday that we get to go to the beach on a Monday?"

"No holiday. Just hanging out time. We haven't done that in a while. I have a ball, we can have a catch or maybe throw the Frisbee."

"How about both?"

"Are you trying to wear me out youngblood?"

"Me, wear you out? I'm just a kid."

"Yeah right."

After an hour and a half of throwing the ball and running after the Frisbee, it was time to tell Ethan about Dijon. We headed to the concession stand to grab a soda.

"This coke tastes real good dad, real good."

I looked at my watch, it was 4:20, Mangello had already closed. The deal was done.

"Ethan, I need to tell you something."

"First, can I get a re-fill on this coke?"

"Sure." And off he ran to the counter.

The phone rang. It was Mangello. I was about to hear what I didn't want to hear.

"Hello Frank. Are you feeling better?"

"No. Absolutely not. In fact, the opposite. I feel horrible."

"Why? What's going on?"

"Dijon didn't show up."

"What did you say?"

"You heard me right. Dijon didn't show up. There was no answer at his office and his cell phone rings but no answer. No one has a clue what's happening."

"You're not kidding me, are you?"

"Jake, I'm serious. I'm not kidding you."

"That's good news. At least for me and maybe for you. Frank, you gotta believe. You just gotta believe."

"I hear you. Jake hurry up and get that big closing of yours done will you?"

"I'm going for it."

"Let me know when you know something."

"I sure will Frank. Count on it."

Ethan returned as I shut off the phone.

"So what do you have to tell me dad?"

A million things flashed through my mind as I was trying to get a grasp on what I just heard.

"Dad? Earth to my father."

"I'm sorry Ethan. What did you say?"

"You said you were going to tell me something

when I got back from getting my re-fill. I'm back, so you can tell me."

"Ethan. I just want you to know that you are the best kid on the planet and I'm so glad you are my son. I love you so very much."

"I know that dad but what were you going to tell me?"

"Sometimes, when you're in a big game and you've losing by a couple of runs in the last inning with two outs, and it sure doesn't look like there's any chance you can win the game, well then …you just gotta keep believing."

CHAPTER 35

Moe's Place looked like Times Square on New Years Eve but Blackie's table sat empty and he was nowhere in sight. It was five days since I heard from him. That wasn't normal. What was normal was when I sat down at Blackie's table, a bunch of eyes glared at me. But when the waitress recognized me and came over, they all calmed down. Some things don't change.

"Want something to drink while you wait for Blackie?"

"Decaf works."

She brought it to me in less than a minute. Five minutes later she came back to refill it.

"He's late today. What's up? Where's he been?" she asked me.

"I was going to ask you the same question."

"It's been days since he's been here," she said shaking her head. "That's not like him."

"I guess we'll have to wait to find out."

"You want to order some food while you wait?"

"Maybe in a few minutes."

I waited another fifteen minutes before I called him. His phone rang and this time he answered.

"Man, I'm sorry Jake. I forgot to call you. I meant to. You're sitting at my table right?"

"You got it. Where the hell are you? I've been trying to reach you for days. You been drunk?"

"No. No nothing like that. Besides I can't drink and drive?"

"Drive? Where the hell are you?"

"I'm about thirty minutes away from the entrance to the Holland Tunnel."

"The Holland Tunnel? The Holland Tunnel like in New Jersey?"

"You got it."

"What the hell are you doing there?"

"Jake I couldn't take it anymore. Hanging out with Ethan just made me want my own kid more. I just had to see him."

"So when you coming back?"

"I'm not."

"Horse shit, you're not."

"Buddy, here's the bottom line. I was sitting at home drinking a beer and it hit me like a ton of New York city bricks. 'I gotta get out of here!' So I got a u-haul trailer, brought the stuff I didn't want to Goodwill, loaded up with what I wanted and hit the road. "

"Why didn't you let me know?"

"I didn't want to have second thoughts. I just had to do it. I was going to let you know when I got here."

"I'm happy for you but I would have understood and would've helped you."

"No need for help. I was a focused demon. Besides you have your hands full with the idiot Dijon. What's happening with that?"

"Mangello called me. He said Dijon didn't show up at the closing yesterday and nobody knows where he is."

"That doesn't surprise me. With guys like that you never know what can happen. Sometimes life just catches up with them. One day poof, they're gone, never to be seen again. There's no telling. And how's your deal coming."

I gave him the particulars and finished with the hope that the deal would get done.

"Jake my boy, I'm rooting for you. You deserve it."

"Yeah, I keep telling myself I gotta believe and I keep rehearsing my happy ending."

"Hey buddy boy, traffic is getting really hairy right now. I need to pay better attention. Gotta go. Let me know when you know. Okay?"

"You got it."

The waitress came over. "Is he coming?"

"Not today. Not tomorrow. But I'd like to order breakfast."

I ate slowly and mindfully. I'd grown to like Moe's Place but I doubted I'd be back, unless for some reason, I wanted to revisit Blackie's place.

***

An hour later I walked into Office Depot when my phone rang. It was Joe Shapiro.

"What's up Joe?"

"Jake, Shapiro here."

"I know. What's up?"

"We got that asshole of a brother straightened out. The documents will arrive tomorrow. So we want to set the closing up for the next day, Thursday. And this time I hope your buyer shows up with the cash to close. I will raise holy hell if he doesn't. Do you understand?"

I had enough of Shapiro but didn't see much point in letting him have it between his eyes but I felt I needed to state my position. I said calmly and softly.

"Joe can you hear me?"

"Yeah I can hear you. What?"

"Joe Shapiro can you hear me?"

"I said yes. Yes I can hear you," he blustered.

"Good. I don't react well to threats. Not at all. Now, do you understand?"

There was no response from Shapiro.

"I assume you understand, Joe. I will call Street's office and be there at closing with the money. Good bye."

As soon as I hung up I called Marshall Deacon. No answer, so I left him a message. Then I considered calling Miriam Nemeth but remembered that she was out of the country and I had no way to connect with her but through Deacon. I figured I'd done what I could. It had been a strange week. I just kept imagining and believing my happy ending.

CHAPTER 36

When I arrived at Street's office for the closing, I was mentally and emotionally prepared for the deal to close. When I went to bed the previous night I meditated on being Onederful, rehearsed my happy ending and fell asleep repeating, "Thank you, thank you, thank you." In the morning, I did it all again. I was ready to leave the closing table with a big, fat check. I felt it in my bones.

I was escorted into the empty conference room and given a cup of decaf. After a few minutes I heard sharp banter coming down the hall toward the conference room. Axelrod and Shapiro entered the room in mid-sentence.

"...never mind. I'll deal with it when we're done here," Axelrod said to Shapiro.

We exchanged pleasantries and made idle chatter. Minutes later Street entered the room.

"Gentlemen, we have everything we need to close except the buyer's representation and of course, the money, which is what this is all about."

I looked at my watch. " It's only a few minutes past the hour and Mr. Deacon assured me that he will be here."

"I warned you Shaw. I warned you," heaved Shapiro.

I paid no attention to Shapiro's babble but addressed both Axlerod and Street. "I have every reason to believe that Mr. Deacon will be here momentarily."

Forty-five minutes later, the room was filled with palpable tension. I had tried to call Mr. Deacon a couple of times but didn't get a connection. My stomach was bouncing. The good news was that for most of the time Shapiro had kept his mouth shut.

"Let me go outside and call him maybe I can get a better connection."

"God damn it Shaw, I…." Shapiro blurted out before Axelrod yanked on Shapiro's arm, which caused him to shut up.

"I'll be back soon," I said. I hoped with Deacon and the money.

I headed to the elevator, took it to the street level, and went outside hoping for some fresh air and an update from Deacon. I got the fresh air but no update. Now, not only was I concerned but I was also angry. Was Miriam Nemeth on the level? What the hell was this about? I was pissed at myself too for believing in her and in some old man with a bunch of bull shit about spirituality and systems and a Higher Power. What a croc! A huge croc! The only good thing was that Dijon was still missing. Good for me but not for Mangello. And who knew if Dijon would show up with some plausible excuse and still want to close. Mangello would close in a heartbeat and I'd be sunk. But then I caught myself from going down that rabbit hole, got a grip and cancelled my incoming doubt. With mindfulness I centered on being Onederful, persisted in living in my happy ending and repeating, 'Thank you, Thank you, Thank you.' After fifteen futile to faithful minutes, I went back upstairs.

When I get back to the conference room, Shapiro blasted me but this time Axelrod didn't stop him.

"Did you find your invisible attorney with the invisible money Shaw? Where the hell is this character? This is all just a bunch of bull shit. I wouldn't be surprised if you're a looney tune and made this whole thing up. You said you had this under control. Sure, like Custer had Bull Run under control. No wonder you haven't closed a deal in a year. You're so incompetent, it's a wonder you're not living on the street."

When I heard those words I went cold, ice cold. I stood up straight as a steel column. I was doing everything I could to not clock this son of bitch when Axelord raised his voice to Shapiro.

"Joe go outside. Go to the bathroom. Go anywhere just get the hell out of this room."

After Shapiro left the room Axelrod turned to me.

"I admire your control Mr. Shaw. When I was your age I might have handled Shapiro differently, with less restraint so to speak. And quite frankly, I'm sure that you're most capable of handling it in another way as well. But now…do you feel you've done all you can do today to get this deal closed?"

"Quite frankly Mr. Axelrod, I have no idea what else I can do."

Street entered the room looking like a referee signaling the end of a game.

"Gentlemen I'm sorry, but we need to adjourn this meeting. I will hold the $250,000 escrow in my account until next week. But I'll tell you this, I've never seen anyone walk away from this size escrow."

"And please note Mr. Shaw," Axelrod said. "We'll settle it without Shapiro."

"That would be good Mr. Axelrod and thank you. Frankly, I don't understand why you deal with a man like Shapiro." I said.

"My younger sister has the unfortunate experience of being married to him. So, in a way he's family. Succinctly, after this deal ends one way or another, he'll still be sort of family but he will not be handling any more of business dealings. Of that I can assure you."

"Thank you for your explanation. My condolences to you," I said.

"Now back to business Mr. Shaw, do you think this deal will ever close?"

"The most honest thing I can say is that I sure hope so, but I have no idea right now. I spoke with Mr. Deacon yesterday and he assured me he'd be here."

I heard someone coming down the hallway. I hoped it was Deacon but it was Shapiro re-entering the meeting. Axelrod nodded for Shapiro to take a seat. Shapiro obeyed.

"Gentlemen, I'm sorry," Street said, "but I do I need to adjourn this meeting. If the buyer ever shows up with the money, we can begin again.

I mumbled, "Where's my happy ending?"

"I'm sorry but I didn't hear what you said?" asked Axelrod.

"I apologize. I was just mumbling to myself."

The bottom line was there was nothing to say. The three men who had entered the room with hope were leaving with disappointment. I was ready for a long session with Henry. I can only imagine what Axelrod was feeling but Shapiro looked like he was ready to blow out of his skin.

We took the elevator to the street floor. The lobby door opened and before us stood a man dressed in an expensive suit jacket hung over his arm. His sleeves were rolled up and his hands were covered with grease. His right hand held an expensive attaché. With sweat dripping from his face he asked, "Are any of you Jake Shaw?"

"I am."

"Nice to meet you in person. I'm Marshall Deacon. And I'm so sorry to be late but I'm lucky to be here at all. Is it too late to get this deal done?"

After Deacon quickly explained his ineptitude at fixing the flat tire on his foreign rental car on the interstate, while his latest and greatest cell phone lay on the front seat useless with a dead battery, the closing took place as smooth as silk.

As we were leaving the conference room, Axelrod tapped me on my shoulder and asked, "Do you mind if we have a few words in private?"

We stepped back into the room. Axelrod shut the door.

"Mr. Shaw, Jake if I may, I've watched you through this entire process. I admire your aplomb and your honesty as well. I'm sure whoever this Munich Trust is also trusts in your professionalism. As I've told you earlier, Joe will not be doing any other deals for us. And to be perfectly blunt, we have a number of them on the table. May I please have your card? I would like to meet with you and discuss your handling our real estate deals for us. Would you be open to that possibility?"

I handed him my card. "I look forward to meeting with you and…"

Just then Shapiro came through the door. "Just got a call from home. They want to know where we are. I told them, we're on our way."

After Axelrod and Shapiro left, I waited for Deacon to come out of the restroom.

"Jake I want to apologize for my comedy of errors," Deacon said.

"There's no need to apologize. I'm grateful for your heroism, riding in here on a greased white horse and saving the day. You made Hollywood jealous. And you made me a very happy man."

"That's good to hear because I feel confident we'll be doing more deals together in the future. Ms. Nemeth has an astute eye for values in real estate and she is bullish on Sarasota, so I think you'll be a busy and successful realtor. And I'll do my best to show up at the next closing on time and without the grease."

We shook hands and parted ways. I sat in my car and tried to get a handle on what just took place. In a few days I would have in my hand a check for

$393,750. The reality hadn't struck me yet. But I did think of Odin words and bellowed, "Thank you! Thank you! Thank you!"

***

Ten minutes later I pulled into my driveway, and saw the same congratulations banner strung across the portico. This time I was happy to see it. When I opened the front and Camille and Ethan stood there in anxious anticipation. Camille held a glass of bourbon for me.

"I hope this is for a toast of celebration and not to drown our sorrows," she said with a smile.

"Baby, it's for sure a toast of celebration. A big toast of celebration."

"I knew it. I knew it would happen," she said in glee.

"Hooray for dad, we were rooting for you just like you root for me in baseball. I was hoping you'd hit a home run. Did you?"

"You bet I did slugger. Not only did I hit a homer, I hit a grand slammer with two out in the bottom of the ninth inning and we win the World Series."

"Wow! A walk off grand slammer! I'm proud of you dad."

"And I'm proud of you too, darling. You sure made magic happen. And I can make magic happen as soon as I cook the pasta. Anybody hungry around here?"

Both Ethan and I raised our hand like two kids in a classroom.

"Good. You guys clean up and I'll get it started."

"I have two quick phone calls to make. I'll be done before you're finished."

My first one was to Frank Mangello.

"Frank, are you sitting down? I have some great news for you. My deal closed. I have the money to pay off my mortgage free and clear without any discount to you."

I don't hear anything on the other end.

"Frank are you there? Frank? Hello Frank?"

"Yes I'm here Jake. I was trying to hold back my tears so I could talk."

"No need to hold anything back. Monday we'll get together and arrange our own closing and we'll both breathe even better than we are now."

"Jake I don't know what to say but thank you. My wife will be overjoyed as I am."

"We're just as happy. I'm glad that I get to be the one to help you for change. See you Monday. Enjoy your weekend."

Next, I called Blackie.

"Hey Yankee, how you doing?"

"I couldn't be better. I'm sitting here with Bobby eating pizza having a blast. How'd your closing go?"

"A little bumpy at the start but all's well that ends well. And in a few days I'll have a big fat check in my hand. And wherever the bastard Dijon may be, he can kiss my ass."

"Way to go buddy. Way to go. I knew you'd do it. I knew it."

"At times I had my doubts and I know you're not going to buy this but I kept doing what Odin said about just imagining what I want, keep rehearsing my happy ending and not be concerned about how things will be arranged."

"Odin 'shmodin.' Whatever took place, took place. Things happen. Guys like Dijon disappear all the time. Listen to me. Your ship landed from that referral, what's his name?"

"Bill Verzi."

"Verzi. That's what got you this deal. Not some hocus pocus shit. You hear me?"

I laughed and Blackie laughed with me.

"Listen don't let your pizza get cold talking with me. You and Bobby enjoy your time and I'll talk with you soon."

I hung up and I remembered something I read, "For those who believe, there's no proof necessary and for those who don't believe, there's no proof possible."

For me the proof was in the pudding and I had the pudding.

"Come on dad, the pasta is ready. I'm starving."

CHAPTER 37

A week after my closing, Mangello was paid off and I owned my home free and clear. It felt so damn good. Life was great except for one thing. I hadn't been able to talk with Odin. Every single morning I'd gone to the park and no sign of Odin. Something wasn't right. There was a void, a sense he really wasn't here any longer. I wondered if he died.

I was coming to the end of my fourth lap around the half-mile loop when I realized I needed to expand my search for Odin beyond the park and Charlie's News Stand. I wanted to see if I could find where he lived. I remembered he said something about condominiums, so I walked across Tamiami Trail and down Gulfstream Blvd. About half mile down Gulfstream I came up to the St. Francis, a fourteen story condominium and I felt an intuitive nudge. A moving truck was parked in front. The truck's loading ramp was fully extended. I couldn't tell if someone was moving in or moving out. I went to the entrance door, it was held open by a brick. I entered. Across the lobby the elevator door opened and two burly moving men exited. I acted like I lived there.

"Do we have someone moving in or moving out?"

A brusque answer came from the older man, "Out. Penthouse."

"Thanks. Good to know."

I played a hunch, entered the vacant elevator and hit the PH button. The ride up was quick, the doors opened onto a small but elegant lobby where a man with a bunch of keys turned and looked at me.

"Can I help you?" he asked.

Surprised by his presence I mentally stumbled but recovered quickly.

"You look like a guy who might be able to do just that. I might be totally lost, even in the wrong building but I'm looking for a friend of mine. A tall elderly gentleman,"

"Buddy, that doesn't narrow it down any," he said.

"His name is Odin."

"Odin. Why didn't you say so? Sure I know Odin. Should say I knew Odin."

"Knew Odin?"

"Yeah, he was a great guy. He departed us last week. This is the unit where he lived. The moving crew is emptying it."

"Did you say departed? Like died?"

The man laughed, "Odin die. That's a joke. That old guy will out live all of us. Die no, he just moved out."

"Where did he move? Do you know how I can get in touch with him?"

"I'm only the superintendent here, but even if I

knew I couldn't tell you. Privacy stuff, you know."

"Maybe someone else could help me?"

"Well here's the thing Mac. Odin didn't own the condo. He was just staying here for a couple of months. The woman who owned it died just after he moved in. There's no record of him ever being here that I know and she certainly can't tell you anything any more. Sorry Mac, I think you're out of luck."

"Thanks anyway."

Nevertheless for the next two weeks, out of raw hope that Odin might show up at the park, I ran the Bay Front Park loop at 8:30 a.m. but without a glimmer of Odin. Like Elvis, Odin had left the building.

***

Two weeks later, I sat shivering in the air-conditioned ice box called the Sarasota airport, waiting for a prospect to arrive from Ohio. I leafed through the property sheets that I had selected for him to see. It was early morning and the airport was still quiet except for the public address system blaring information on the imminent departure of a flight to New York. The second time it was announced it was even louder. I continued to look through my sheets. A few moments later the third announcement seemed to scream directly at me. I looked up annoyed, attempting to understand the reason for its tone and I saw a tall elderly man on the other side of the security gate walking quickly toward the boarding gate. It was Odin. I sprang to my feet, the papers dropping off my lap. Immediately I called, "Odin!"

He stopped walking and turned toward me with a smile on his face. He pointed his index finger directly at me, then gave me a thumbs up sign and winked at me.

Seeing him made my eyes water. I heaved a big sigh of relief. Then I gave him a wide smile, put my clasped hands to my chest, bowed my head slightly and whispered, Thank you. Thank you. Thank you."

Brian A. Hill
is an author, metaphysician and
entrepreneur who has written
for the New York Times, Halifax
Media and Gatehouse Media.
He lives in Sarasota, Florida

41300292R00158

Made in the USA
San Bernardino, CA
09 November 2016